Return to Pentwater

MARTHA ROBACH

Other Books by Martha Robach:

The Charlevoix Greats
https://www.createspace.com/3337793

The Forbidden Gold of Mackinac
https://www.createspace.com/3725004

Also available on Amazon and Kindle

Follow on Facebook under Mitten Moments,

Return to Pentwater, The Charlevoix Greats,

The Forbidden Gold of Mackinac

Twitter @MarthaRobach

DEDICATION

To Tom for his gentle support; and to God, whose daily gifts ever amaze.

CONTENTS

1 AUGUST

It was the middle of August, which brought with it mid-August things: end-of-season sales at the gift shops and hazy, muggy days topped by dry, papery-green leaves. And though the harbor still churned with growling power boats and sleek sliding sailboats, a quiet knowledge hung over the little lakeside berg of Pentwater, Michigan, like a mist. A change of season was due.

Chloe Hening pushed on the heavy wooden screen door of "Art at Pentwater," stepping into the hot ripe sunshine.

"Thanks, Mrs. Chartel," she called out over her shoulder. "I'll be back next week."

Chloe paused, carefully placing the "Art at Pentwater" receipts into a large briefcase. With her shiny ponytail, casual top and jean shorts, Chloe didn't look like a bookkeeper, except for the battered briefcase she lugged from store to store. Talk in Pentwater was that Chloe Hening had become a most attractive woman as she reached her 27th birthday. This was surprising, since her earlier years had been less than promising.

The shy, skinny girl with mouse-brown hair had filled out, ever so slightly, streaked her hair either by bottle or the sun—it was hard to tell which—and brought attention to her very blue eyes with the careful use of mascara. With these outward changes came more confidence and poise. But, of course, she *was* 27 and no longer a child. The shop owners still felt a jolt when those blue eyes twinkled at them in adult-to-adult jest. They remembered the little girl tucked behind her father's legs or trudging, head down, around corners on her way to school. But now they trusted her with their books, their very livelihoods, and with good reason, for Chloe was an excellent bookkeeper.

It seems she was born to take care of finances. In her teens she was always hanging around her father as he grumbled his way through the accounts at Manitou Inn, the resort hotel he owned and ran. Each year she handled more of Manitou Inn's accounting chores until, at 18, Chloe took over entirely. Her father's bragging about her—and the fact Manitou Inn was thriving—led other Pentwater business owners to entrust Chloe with their books. For this reason, without the benefit of college, Chloe was well-employed. Since her clients were generally seasonal businesses, her work dropped sharply in the fall and started up again during tax season. But fall was the time for repairs at Manitou Inn, where Chloe lived with her father and her sister's child, Lilli.

As Chloe trudged down the street, briefcase in tow, her fingers patted the pocket of her shorts to feel the crispness of the letter she had just picked up from the post office. It was an official notice that Braden Willis from Willis Properties, Inc., would arrive in Pentwater on Friday, exactly four days later, to talk to Chloe and her father about updating Manitou Inn and making it part of their chain of hotels.

Chloe paused as she reached Manitou Inn and tried to analyze it impersonally. The summer home of an industrial baron from Chicago, with five turrets and a huge pillared portico—neighborhood children dubbed it "the castle"—it was built in 1904. Manitou Inn was an architect's dream and a handyman's nightmare. It was a nightmare especially for her also aging father, now 60, who had purchased it for a song 25 years ago and done extensive remodeling that was now showing some fray around the edges.

Chloe sighed and marched in the front door, past the visitor's lounge and through the door in back of the front desk that led to the family's living area.

"Hi, Pops," she called, flinging her briefcase onto a worn green brocade sofa.

A muffled "Whazzat" from the kitchen led Chloe there, only to see her father belly up under the sink, his legs jerking with the effort of tightening a pipe.

"Pops, you know you're not supposed to be doing that. Where's Charlie?"

"How do I know? Resting under a tree, I suppose," came the muttered reply. "Dad-gummed rotten pipe keeps breaking."

Chloe half bent over. It was useless to argue with her father.

"Well, can I run to the hardware store for some more rotten pipes or joints?"

"No. Someone has got to cover the desk. Find that lazy nincompoop Charlie, wherever he's hiding, and send *him* to help me."

"I'll call him," Chloe said. "Don't worry. I'll cover the desk."

As soon as Charlie had been dispatched and Chloe answered a few phone calls and gave extra towels to guests in Room 10, Lilli walked through the door, fresh from her art class.

"How was Mr. Weatherspoon, darlin'?"

"Mean. But we drew birds. Want to see?"

Blowing up the dark bangs sticking to her forehead, Lilli pulled out charcoal sketches of birds in flight from her portfolio that looked—well, in their accuracy and proportion, nothing like the drawings of an 8-year-old. More astounding was how Lilli caught the motion of flight.

Chloe sighed. "Beautiful, beautiful."

"Oh, they're really not that good," Lilli said, sniffing. "And he didn't give me time to finish. Can I go to the beach, Chloe? Then I'll watch the birds and sketch some. Can I go if I promise to stay out of the water?"

Chloe looked wistfully at Lilli's wide, shining brown eyes.

"Lunch first, sweetie. Maude's waiting for you in the kitchen with your peanut butter sandwich. I don't want you at the beach alone. And Grandpa's busy. How about if I take you at 2:00 p.m., when I'm done posting this account?"

"Okay."

And with a "Maude, I'm home," Lilli unceremoniously dropped her portfolio and sprinted for the kitchen.

Chloe settled her briefcase on the worn desk, thinking how much she too needed a walk on the beach, to dig her toes into the hot sand and watch the gulls flying through the blue fathomless sky while Lilli drew. She only wished the closeness she felt to God and the peace she experienced by the lake extended back to the house with her accounts. But no matter. They had to be done. She opened her ledger book decisively.

Later, after she and Lilli splashed in the waves and fed the gulls part of a bag of stale bread that Lilli was using now to entice the birds close enough to draw, Chloe lay back on the beach blanket and closed her eyes.

Lilli and the secret. Chloe thought of it more and more lately. She couldn't help feeling keeping the secret hurt Lilli, no matter how good the intentions were of its instigator, Lilli's mother.

What a black impact that summer nine years ago had on her family, with the exquisite exception of Lilli who, by her very nature, must be a treasure always. It all began when Lilli's father, a painter—a married painter—

arrived in Pentwater for a summer. He came to paint water colors of Pentwater and Lake Michigan, as well as give his two school-age children a vacation while his socialite wife visited Europe with her parents. Chloe was 18 then; her older sister Marie, 20. Chloe and Marie often babysat his children at the beach while he would set up his easel and paint. His painting was exceptional; his personality even more so. The stories he told! Just being around him made life an exciting adventure. He was always "on," always alert, always living, with his dark penetrating eyes and shock of unruly black hair. Even Chloe felt the electricity surrounding him, though she was dating Mark that summer. But it was Marie who began to worry her.

It was so unlike Marie, serious and responsible, the one who took over as mother when Chloe's mom, who suffered from a weak heart, had an "attack". Chloe could feel the joyful glow radiating from her sister when this artist fellow was around. She could read the love in her sister's eyes because that was the summer of Mark, when Chloe's heart too was full of the exhilaration first love brings. But David Trassault was a 35-year-old man, a husband, a father. Nothing good awaited her sister there, Chloe knew. And Chloe's feelings for Mark—indeed that whole summer—were affected, tinged with the darkness of the passion that was engulfing her sister.

Her parents, busy and oblivious, didn't notice their elder daughter's absorption with this guest. So Chloe could only look on anxiously as David laughed, painted, told stories and played his guitar to the soft smiles of Marie and watch them come together like a magnet. Her fears became certainty when she caught the two of them in a tight embrace on a moonlight stroll after putting his children to bed.

David and his children left Manitou Inn during the second week of August, but by then the damage was done. Chloe watched her sister suffer in summer's mellow aftermath. But Marie was silent until November, when she informed her astonished parents she was pregnant. Pops' angry demand that David be told of his baby only made Marie more stubborn. She wouldn't hurt David and his marriage. And in the end she made the family give a solemn promise that David should never know about Lilli. How that vow would have been kept had Marie not died of a blood clot three days after Lilli's birth, Chloe had no way of knowing. But since it was Marie's last request, the family felt it should be honored. Her death sealed their vow. Unfortunately, it also, in effect, made Lilli an orphan, an orphan without cause.

Chloe watched the thin little girl with the long dark curls sketch demurely with one hand while with the other hand she scattered bread crumbs for the gulls. If only David had come back to Manitou Inn, he would have known in an instant this was his daughter, so strong was the resemblance. This must be truly fate, for they heard nothing from him in the nine years since the summer of Lilli's conception.

One hour stretched into two until Chloe and Lilli at last departed, after a final wallow in the waves to replace the sand grains with water droplets which cooled the sun's fry on their block-long walk home.

When they arrived, her father was cutting bushes in the front yard.

"Pops," Chloe called. "It's too hot for that. Give it an hour to cool down, and I'll do it."

Uncharacteristically, her father laid down the clippers and headed, red-faced and perspiring, for the house.

"You're right. I'm exhausted. I think I'll take a nap."

Later in the twilight, when the bushes had taken their toll on her in scratches, woodsy fragments and sweat, Chloe grabbed the letter from her dresser and headed downstairs to find her father. He was tucked in his armchair watching TV. Lilli had gone to Maude's for the night, to further her tight companionship with Maude's granddaughter, Melanie, over Barbie dolls and videos.

"Got the letter today, Pops," she said.

"What letter?"

"Oh, you know, from Willis Properties. They're sending Braden Willis up on Friday to talk to us."

"Great. Some big-time Chicago schmuck trying to steal our business out from under us."

"Or saving you from an early demise fretting about this place."

"Well, my blood pressure is going to skyrocket when they come in here and ruin everything."

"Oh, Pops," Chloe said with a sigh. "We've been through this before. You know running the hotel is too much for you now that you're older and alone. It was hard enough when Mom was living and you two were in your forties."

"I just can't stand strangers telling me what to do, with all their newfangled ideas."

"Give them a chance. Okay? I mean a *real* chance, because you need help desperately, and you know it. I'm surprised Charlie hasn't quit on you by now."

With a grunt of disapproval, her father resumed his TV show. Chloe hoped this Braden Willis was a good salesman, because he would have a tough sell convincing her father to agree to a partnership with his chain of hotels where they would renovate, help run the hotel and make it part of their advertised chain for a 50/50 profit split.

2 BRADEN WILLIS

Early Friday morning a thunderstorm with heavy rains rolled through and broke the heat of the early week. It left clear, brilliant skies and upper 70s temperatures, a welcome relief. Chloe lingered at her upper bedroom window, fingering the filmy curtains and waiting for Braden Willis to arrive. Promptly at 9:00 a.m. an apple-red Jaguar convertible skidded to a stop in the hotel's driveway and a tall young man stepped out and headed towards the front door.

"Pops, he's here," Chloe called.

When the door bell rang, she took the steps two at a time. She pulled open the door and stifled a gasp. Before her stood possibly the best-looking man she had ever seen. He was tall, at least 6 foot 3 inches, with large green eyes flecked with hazel, and a beautifully sculpted nose and mouth. His hair was light brown, straight, thick, shiny and brushed back in an impeccably trimmed haircut. He wore a suit and tie, full business regalia, and immediately held out his hand.

"Hi. I'm Braden Willis."

"Chloe Hening. Won't you come in?"

Her father loomed behind her. As proper introductions began, Chloe wondered with chagrin how she must appear to this well turned out individual of her approximate age—a small-town hick, no doubt.

A glance up to discover his attitude was all it took to see the impression she made on him was very good. His eyes kept fixing on her. He looked slightly bewildered, as though unsure of what he would say next. This in someone of so favorable an appearance made Chloe turn a childish glowing pink.

"So ... you've lived here all your life?" he brought out, forgetting the business before them.

"Yes. And you're from Chicago?"

At this point Chloe's father looked in disgust from one to the other.

"Well, look me up when you're finished with pleasantries. In fact, look me up when you've got the whole deal worked out because, no matter what she says, you know who the real boss is here." And, with that, he spun around and left the room.

Chloe sighed and flushed some more. How like her father to back out at the last minute, leaving her in charge. But it was for the best, she supposed. There would be so many details to thrash out without his obvious negativity.

She looked up at Braden Willis, who was still staring at her with this kind of warmth behind his eyes.

"I've got parents too."

"I'm so sorry, Mr. Willis."

"Braden, please."

"Braden. He's not happy about doing this. But, believe me, we really need some help."

"I totally understand. My father is the same; wants to do everything his way."

"Your father, as in Willis Properties?"

"Yes. He's the CEO. I have the dubious honor of working for my father."

"Then we share that; me in my small way," Chloe added.

"The problems are probably remarkably similar,"

Braden said, still smiling and looking into her eyes.

Chloe returned his smile, flushing once more. *What's wrong with me?* she thought. *I'm acting like a schoolgirl.* It couldn't be just his looks; more his obvious admiration that was disconcerting her.

"Where shall we begin?" she said, trying to pull herself together.

"I have our whole program right here," he said, pulling a booklet out of his briefcase. "Why don't I go over this with you? And, when we're done, you can tell me your concerns."

"Begin at the beginning?"

"Exactly," he said, smiling.

Because he was using a booklet and he only had one, Chloe ended up sitting next to him on the living room couch. Normally such a thing wouldn't have discomfited her. But she couldn't help smelling his aftershave and noticing his ring finger was bare.

"Mind if I remove my jacket? It's stifling in here."

"Of course not." Well-muscled arms, slightly hairy—she had to stop this.

Though Braden Willis spread the laminated paper before Chloe and began describing his company's incorporation program, he was showing noticeable signs of distraction, a fact which did not escape Chloe and, in truth, caused her a considerable amount of delight.

He thinks he *has problems*, Chloe thought. *What am I going to do when it is my turn to ask intelligent questions?*

Suddenly he stopped his spiel in mid-sentence. "Chloe, forgive me. This is a great program, and I'm not doing it justice right now. Could we return to this later when I've got my act together? What about lunch?"

She stood up. "There's a nice place by the pier."

"Spare no expense; my treat."

In seconds they were walking together in the heat and the sunshine, Braden having quickly pulled off his tie as he had his sports jacket earlier.

Chloe glanced ruefully at her jean shorts.

"I probably should have changed."

"*Never*," Braden said emphatically. "You look perfect the way you are."

Chloe hoped the warmth she felt at his words was not showing again in her cheeks. It was ridiculous, this blushing. She couldn't remember the last time she had this problem.

"In fact, I want to remember you this way, the first time I saw you."

"Oh," she said with a nervous giggle, "now you're flattering me."

"I never flatter," he replied earnestly, looking directly into her eyes. "In fact, you have absolutely floored me, Chloe, and I think you know it. And I'm 32, not 16. So that's what makes it unusual, I think."

After they had been seated, he leaned toward her and said, "So tell me about yourself. Why are you here instead of Chicago or some other urban sprawl?"

"Oh, I love it here," Chloe said.

"But aren't the winters dull?"

Chloe found it hard to describe the silent windswept bleakness of the beach or the serenity of Pentwater in winter. It would sound ridiculous, she knew, from his perspective, yet she felt it deeply.

"No," she said simply. "I find them beautiful."

He smiled. "Then beautiful they are. But what about the big city, the clubs, the night life?"

"I have no experience with any of that, I'm afraid," Chloe said with a sigh.

"That should change, then. I definitely want you to come to Chicago."

Chloe couldn't help smiling at that.

"I mean it. You'll love Chicago. So much is happening."

"I guess I'm smiling at now decisive you sound."

"No. You'll love it. And I want you to understand I'm not trying to sell you anything. This is strictly personal.

I want you to come to Chicago whether or not your father buys into our company."

"Oh, Chicago sounds exciting. But I have to say I love life in Pentwater. Lilli keeps things interesting."

"Lilli?"

"My sister's daughter, my niece. She lives with Pops and I."

"And where is your sister?"

"She died from childbirth complications."

"How terrible. But what about her father? I don't see how he could just leave her," Braden continued, a scowl creasing his elegant brow.

Braden was probing an open wound, and it took all the strength Chloe had to answer in a hoarse whisper.

"Well, it was a summer romance, and her father was ... married, an artist, I guess. We're not sure where he is now."

It wasn't really a lie but, again, not the full truth, and Chloe hated saying it. Lately she felt there was no excuse for Lilli not knowing her father apart from the fact that her father might not want to acknowledge Lilli. But shouldn't such a monumental decision be left between father and daughter?

Chloe's darkened look made Braden veer off the subject of Lilli's father. He shook his head ruefully and grinned.

"I'm afraid I have little experience with children, even at my advanced age."

Chloe's face brightened. "Well, Lilli is our angel. She's easy. In fact, she's the light of Pops' and my life. And Maude, our head housekeeper, takes Lilli home with her so often she has a bed at her house. It's a patchwork-quilt life for Lilli, but she seems happy. She's so good in art she has advanced lessons, which are hard to come by in Pentwater. Luckily a retired painter who lives here was willing to take her on."

"She sounds like a remarkable little girl. But now I want to hear about her remarkable aunt."

"Oh, I don't know. I graduated from Pentwater High and started doing the books for my father and some other businesses in town. I love living by the beach; my life in a nutshell, I guess."

"Are you involved with anybody now?"

"Nobody special," she said, smiling.

"And why are you smiling? Was there somebody 'special'?"

"A long time ago, back in high school."

"But you've kept your distance since then?"

"I guess you could say that. Living in a resort town, I seem to meet summer visitors, maybe guests here or in town. And then they leave at summer's end, and we have some contact by phone or weekends up here or down wherever. But, you know, by the next summer invariably it's over. And I'm usually ready for it to be over."

"I hope you don't think you'll get rid of *me* so easily."

"I do meet a lot of people from Chicago. You could say I know the city well, not so much by a weekend visit as by its people."

"I hope you're not prejudiced about us Chicagoans," Braden said with a smile.

"Well, since Chicago has been good to us customer-wise, I'm not saying a word," Chloe said with an ironic grin. "You don't fight with your clients if you're smart."

"Ouch. Don't think I want to go any further with that. I get your point. But with any luck, I'll be the exception to the rule."

After they finished lunch, Braden excused himself.

"Chloe, hang on for a second. I'm going to call my hotel on the cell phone and arrange for a couple more nights. And if you're agreeable, let's go back to the hotel and get your father. I think I can give both of you a few points to think about today and discuss the input you have on them tomorrow. I'm fired up again."

Braden was right about being fired up because, after his presentation, Chloe could see her father was impressed. Or maybe relieved would be a better word. Pops was still talking as Braden backed out the front door three hours later.

When the door finally closed, he turned to Chloe. "Though I hate to admit it, you were right about Willis Properties. And that young fellow was sharp. Did you notice his ideas for renovating the place? A keen eye, I'd say."

"Well, don't get too excited," Chloe cautioned. "Maybe they'll back out when they realize how much renovation we need."

"Hmmph," her father responded. "This place is a gem, and they know it."

"Well, the location is excellent," Chloe agreed. "But I don't recall you using such words when you were repairing the pipes the other day."

"Now *they* can worry about that," Pops said with a grunt. "But did you hear him say we would still be in charge of the day-to-day operation of the hotel?"

"You want that, Pops?"

"Of course. Who else gives customer service like we do?"

Chloe knew this is what was bothering her father, entrusting "his" hotel to people who would damage the high standards he had kept at the hotel for so many years.

"Get your questions ready for tomorrow at 9:00 a.m., Pops. Braden said he's going to call the home office and he'll have more figures for us."

"I'll be ready. Don't you worry," Pops said with a mischievous grin. But Chloe could see he was pleased.

"And I promised I'd show him around Pentwater. So don't talk to him all afternoon."

"Oh, perish the thought of my interfering with your social life."

"No. But he should see Pentwater, shouldn't he?"

"And I wasn't born yesterday," Pops said with a dismissive wave of his hand, heading toward the front desk. "Luckily, you're old enough to mess up your personal life any way you see fit."

She wondered if that was an oblique reference to what happened to Marie, because Chloe had had little of substance in the relationship department for years. What little mention Chloe and Pops made of Marie had stopped almost entirely after Chloe's mother passed away three years after Lilli's birth and Marie's untimely death, presumably from a weak heart and perhaps a broken heart as well. Raising a baby and running a hotel had been too much for Mom.

Now they were both gone. Though holding onto some fuzzy memories of Grandma, Lilli had been too young to miss either.

We're a remnant of what used to be a whole family, Chloe thought. *Lilli knows nothing else. And Pops and I are silent, avoiding open wounds that still exist and perhaps always will.*

Mom and Marie were with God now, missed but safe. And, through God's kindness, the Hening remnant on earth was lively and functioning. Chloe felt this was due to their active faith. There was no question where Pops, Chloe and Lilli spent their Sunday mornings. Church was home, and its people a comfort. Through their support, Pops had moved physically, if not altogether emotionally, from grieving his wife and daughter to loving and raising his granddaughter. Chloe found comfort both from Pops' solid grounding and the enjoyment of Pentwater's natural beauty and serenity. And, Lilli, with her artistic sensitivity and translucent questions about eternity, was a total joy.

Yes, we're doing okay, Chloe thought.

But what about Braden Willis, this well-favored young man from a distant metropolis? He made Chloe flustered and flattered, something she had not felt since Mark, since Mark long ago. Suddenly tomorrow looked more interesting, and he was the reason.

3 FIRST IMPRESSIONS

The next morning, Braden arrived in tan shorts and a pastel polo shirt, lugging a huge briefcase and eyes alight. He had obviously done a lot of work in his hotel room the night before, calling the home office, and had some solid figures for the renovation. Pops listened attentively, asked pertinent questions and seemed to grow happier and more relaxed by the minute. Chloe had been impressed by the synopsis she received from Willis Properties before Braden's arrival. They seemed to treat the hotel owner with dignity and trust. And, of course, the profits lost from the incorporation were recouped in the renovation.

"Thank you, Braden," Pops said, shaking his hand. "I guess it's time for me to leave sole ownership of Manitou Inn."

"You won't regret it, Mr. Hening," Braden replied, "not when you see the improvements. And we work in over 100 co-partnerships. So we know what we're doing."

"I can see that. And now I'll let you go. I believe Chloe has plans for you this afternoon."

"Oh, Pops," Chloe said, rolling her eyes.

"That's right," Braden said with a wink. "In fact, I have extended my stay for a couple more days in honor of Pentwater's 'beautiful scenery,'" he said, looking at

Chloe. "And I'll be back next weekend with my front-runner team to take measurements. Then we can start the renovation gradually in the fall, leaving some rooms open for fall color tours."

"Sounds great. Now, go, go," Pops said, waving his hands in dismissal.

Chloe ducked into the kitchen, emerging with a beach bag and picnic basket.

"Let me help you with that," Braden said, shouldering the picnic basket.

"Chloe and her beach paraphernalia," Pops said with a laugh. "She has it down to a science. Hope you brought your swimsuit."

"I bought one yesterday in town. It's in the car. I thought I might be needing it," Braden said with a wink for Chloe.

Chloe took his arm. "There's a changing pavilion on the beach."

"Chloe is in a hurry," Pops teased. "She doesn't want to waste a minute of another lazy day in the sun."

"Don't believe him, Braden," Chloe said, getting into his car, "not the way I work around here."

Braden was silent on the short drive to the beach. They parked the car, changed into their suits and found a good spot on the sand near Lake Michigan. After spreading on a lot of sunscreen and adjusting their beach towels, they both reclined and closed their eyes, blocking the sun's rays and feeling the soft sand mold to their bodies under the towels.

"I don't know about the 'lazy' part," Braden murmured. "But I haven't felt so care-free in a long time. Being with you is relaxing."

"Well, this *is* quite a change from Chicago."

"And I've assigned myself a mini-vacation I hadn't planned on, today and tomorrow. I hope you'll spend tomorrow with me too, Chloe. Or am I being pushy?" he asked, propping his head up on one elbow.

"I'd love to spend tomorrow with you," Chloe replied,

squinting up at him. "Anything I need to do can wait one more day."

"Then I leave Monday morning. But I'll be back next Saturday. And the funny thing is I know I'll miss you, Chloe. Will you miss me?"

Chloe looked away. This was too much too soon. "I don't know what to say. You do have an energizing, awakening kind of effect on me, not at all the peaceful feeling you mentioned."

He laughed, looking down at her, his white even teeth glinting in the sunlight.

"Well, I'll take that as a good sign. But, then again, you certainly don't put me to sleep either."

As he lay back and closed his eyes, Braden's hand reached out and covered Chloe's where it rested on the towel, and they were silent.

That night they went to a small club to dance where Braden caused quite a stir among Chloe's friends, who ogled and came up to be introduced and gather gossip.

As they danced through a slow song, Braden whispered, "Is that high school love of yours here tonight, Chloe?"

"No. He lives in Detroit. We broke up the summer after our senior year," she added.

"Was that the summer of your sister's romance with that artist?"

Chloe looked at him in amazement. "Yes. Why?"

"I just wondered," he said thoughtfully.

Did Braden suspect, as she had, that Marie's misguided passion is what caused she and Mark to part that summer? Had they separated to avoid further spectacle and speculation about the Hening family? At 18 they were too young to be sure of their own emotions. Whatever the reason, Chloe still had regrets about Mark.

"You look sad thinking about him," Braden said, gazing down at her.

"I miss the boy. We grew up together and were best

friends for as long as I can remember. We only started dating that May after the senior prom. And by the end of summer it was over. Three months and I lost my best friend. If we had stayed just friends, we'd be friends today."

"Not necessarily, if he had married and you look as good as you do now," Braden said with a laugh. "*Is* he married, by the way?"

"Yes, to a girl he met at college. His family attend our church. So I get all the details. They're very proud of him. He's an engineer now, I guess."

"But you haven't seen him?"

"No, not in ages."

"Never comes back to visit?"

"He might. But I don't know about it."

"Good," Braden said with a smug nod of his head.

Chloe laughed.

"Now, tell me about *your* romantic past," she said, to change the subject. "You've left a trail of broken hearts, I suppose?"

"Well, I don't know about that," he said, turning serious. "But *my* heart has never been—broken, that is. And at 32 to be so …'unmoved' is a little scary."

"So you decide to fall for the next woman you meet?" Chloe teased.

Braden's eyebrows arched gracefully. "I respect myself too much to do that. But before I saw you standing in that doorway, all the women I met were cookie-cutter copies of each other; well turned out, sophisticated, brittle socialites."

"Well, now I am insulted. By that you're implying *I'm* not well turned out or sophisticated?"

"Not heavily made up with every hair in place and a snotty attitude is more like it."

"Well, I'll admit I've made tousled an art form, but you'd better quit while you're behind," Chloe said with a laugh.

"You're as fresh and pretty as a summer's day," he

murmured, holding her chin up with his finger and giving her such a warm look that her cheeks blossomed again. It was obvious he meant it, that she outstripped the Chicago women he had met, and she would tease him about it no more.

The next day, as Braden and Chloe left for a drive down a quiet, picturesque lakeside road Chloe wanted to show him, Braden said, "You spent the whole morning in church, Chloe. What on earth did you *do*? I was afraid you'd been held captive. And we have so little time."

"You could have joined me," Chloe said in soft remonstrance. "And, what we did: first there was the worship service, then coffee time, and after that Bible study. Lilli goes to Sunday School during Bible study and ..."

"Okay. Okay. I get it." Braden said with a wave of his hand. "I'm sorry I'm so impatient. But it's a beautiful day. And I wanted you all to myself."

And for the rest of the afternoon Chloe felt the sun and waves work in harmonious glory. Braden and she fought the frothy wave crests, walked on the grainy, toasty sand, breathed the windswept air, stared at the translucent sky and lived as one with God's glory, hand-and-hand and at peace with each other. Their smiles were reflected in each other's eyes. Braden's kisses were velvety and insistent as he strained Chloe close to him. And she was sad when the afternoon ended and they sat side by side in his car, sandy, wet and very full of each other.

We're living a commercial, Chloe thought dreamily. *Could this be love?*

As if he had read her thoughts, Braden murmured, "I'm falling in love with you, Chloe."

"Me too," breathed Chloe. "I mean"—and they both laughed—"I wish this day would never end," she said in truth.

"It's been perfect, and you're perfect," he said, kissing her again.

But, as Braden's car pulled out of the driveway the next morning, Chloe's main feeling was one of relief.

How quickly a man changes your life, Chloe thought, a bit reluctantly.

The weekdays before Braden's return the next weekend moved swiftly, filled with his daytime calls to Chloe or to her father for information on their business or details about the proposed renovation. Braden proved himself competent and a hard worker. And at night, around 9:00 o'clock the phone would ring. It would be Braden again, this time for Chloe alone. They talked for hours, tying up the private phone line, much to Pops' irritation.

Braden spoke of his dreams of running Willis Properties, the changes he would make, the ideas he had to make it a better business. Since Chloe was involved in running Manitou Inn and in keeping business accounts, they found a common ground and traded ideas freely, gaining new respect for each other. Braden spoke of their "perfect day" and vowed a repetition the next weekend.

"Pray for sunshine, Chloe," he said.

When he talked of that day, Chloe remembered vividly the sun, the waves and his lips on hers. She shivered.

On Thursday afternoon, when the hotel was quiet and Chloe's duties had ended, she looked at Lilli, who was tossing a ball for Edgar the cat in the corner, all the while studying his moves in an intense way.

She's planning her next "cat" picture, Chloe thought fondly, for Lilli viewed the world as an artist does, always "drawing."

"How about a walk down the beach, sweetheart? Your Aunt Chloe could use a break."

"Can I call Melanie?"

Chloe sighed. Gone was the thrill of them being alone. Now a friend was necessary. *Where has the time flown?* Chloe thought.

"Sure, sweetie. I'll wait."

The day was windy and cool, jacket weather that could come at August's end in Michigan. High floating cirrus clouds dashed through crisp blue skies that carried the hint of fall. Though gusts of wind blew occasional swirls of sand into their eyes, Melanie and Lilli played an edgy dance with the waves hitting the shore and looked for "lake refuse": dead bloated fish, driftwood, bottles, globs of seaweed. Thus absorbed, they were oblivious to Chloe, who strode behind them, hands jammed in her pockets and breathing deeply the fresh air.

Oh, God, how wonderful life is, Chloe thought. *We are so blessed here, Pops, Lilli and myself, surrounded by your beautiful creation and enjoying today our health. I need your guidance with Braden. Is he a person to join my path to or to simply share some of life's precious moments with?*

She watched Lilli laughing as she dodged the waves, dark hair streaming in the wind.

And our darling Lilli, keep her near to your heart and give us direction about her father, David. Luckily, Lilli's heavenly father would always be there for her no matter what, a comfort indeed when earthly parents are absent.

Laying on her pillow that night, the wind still spun and swirled in Chloe's head, refreshing her soul. Braden had just called to say he would be there early Saturday morning. Only one day until the weekend. Chloe yawned and fell asleep immediately.

4 A RELATIONSHIP

Saturday proved to be a rough-hewn day, whose main theme seemed to be a rapid return to reality. Braden, ready to move, change, dig in, arrived loaded with diagrams and lists and an assistant who took measurements. Pops met him at the door with a glowering mistrust, apparently forgetting his enthusiasm over Braden's plans, and argued with him over every detail, even those he had agreed to days before.

Chloe's nerves were so frazzled listening to their complaints, Braden's in one ear and Pops' in the other, she put on her rain parka and went outside, sitting on the porch for the longest time.

Then Lilli came out, asking where Pops was, which made Chloe wonder if a murder or two had been committed. She went inside. After some searching, she found Braden and Pops in an upstairs bedroom, drinking beer and sharing a laugh about a bird who built its nest on a window ledge, making the window impossible to open.

"Look, Chloe, our feathered friend prefers windows to trees," Pops said with a chuckle, giving Braden a friendly thump on the back. Braden looked cheerful.

"I never anticipated this problem," he said brightly.

"Er, yeah, sure," Chloe said, backing out of the room. The rest of the afternoon she avoided the two men. They seemed to get along better without her.

But Chloe's biggest problem Saturday came later when Pops and Lilli were in bed and Braden and she were watching TV in the living room. The trouble was Braden had no interest in watching TV. He wound his arms around her and began kissing her lips, her eyes, her neck. Chloe felt herself melting into him. And his lips were awakening such sweet excitement in her she knew where this lovemaking would quickly lead. But she shouldn't, couldn't follow where her senses were taking her. Steeling herself, Chloe pushed against Braden's chest with both hands and struggled up off the couch. Braden immediately jumped up next to her, pulling her body up towards his kisses and edging backward towards the couch again.

"Braden, we have to stop. I mean it," Chloe said, averting her face, her voice edged in panic.

Braden jerked back as if she had struck him.

"I don't understand. We're so good together. Would you rather come back to my hotel room?" he whispered. "I know this might not be the right time or place."

"It isn't that, Braden. Don't you know I'm a Christian? I follow God's laws—or try to, I guess. And right now you seem the epitome of temptation to me."

"But I love you, Chloe," Braden said softly. "Doesn't that make a difference? I'm not like David was to your sister." He appeared truly mystified by her denial.

"I know that, Braden," she said, softly touching his face. "But I believe it's wrong without marriage; not that I'm asking for marriage. But you know what I mean."

"Well, you're a rare one, Chloe. I must say that."

"I knew you were a heartbreaker," Chloe retorted.

Braden was thinking. "Well. Okay. I think I can live with this. The good thing is you haven't been with other men either ... have you?"

"No," Chloe said. Frankly, Chloe found Braden's comments disturbing and somewhat crass. This was not a perfect end to her Saturday evening at all.

A chastened Braden went with Chloe, Pops and Lilli to church the next day. His "perfect" suit and haircut drew all eyes to him. But Braden acted like a fish out of water.

While driving back to Manitou Inn in his car, Braden said, "What do those people in church think, *really* think? I'm betting they just want others to see how good they are."

"You don't know them, Braden, like I do," Chloe countered. "Most of them—not all, I'm sure, but most— love the Lord as I do."

"I'm sorry, Chloe," Braden said, squeezing her hand. "I'm just skeptical."

Chloe pressed his hand in return.

"I understand. You're just not used to church."

"Yeah. It's a real eye-opener."

After church, Lilli, somewhat bored without Melanie, who had gone to town with her parents, snuggled between Braden and Chloe on the couch. She looked at Braden with some interest.

"Are you coming back next weekend, Braden?"

"If I can."

"To see Aunt Chloe and work on the house?"

"Yes."

"Are you and Aunt Chloe going on another ride this afternoon?"

"Yes."

"Where?"

"Along the beach road, this time north, I think."

"Can I come too? I can find some pretty rocks for you."

"Not this time, Lilli; maybe next weekend."

Lilli sighed and looked at Chloe. Then she suddenly jumped off the couch and left the room. Chloe hated to see her hurt or lonely.

"I worry about Lilli, she"...

"I'm sorry, Chloe. I just wanted to see you alone. We have so little time together."

"I know," Chloe said hesitantly. "I just want you and Lilli to be friends."

"Plenty of time for that," Braden said firmly.

Chloe was silent on their drive that afternoon, which ended at a picturesque Italian restaurant in the harbor of a small town north of Pentwater. She was still thinking, worrying about Lilli and wishing they had taken her with them. She knew Braden was unused to children. But she couldn't help resenting his dismissive attitude towards Lilli. To his credit, Braden seemed aware of what was causing her discomfiture.

"You're wishing I was nicer to Lilli, right?" he asked.

"Yes. In most ways she's my own child. Don't you see?"

"I'm truly sorry, Chloe. I have so much to learn about you."

"Lilli, Pops and I have grown so tight because we're all each other has had. We're a package deal, no less."

Braden looked solemn. "I can see that. But we also need time alone, Chloe, especially now when I'm leaving tonight for Chicago again. Can't you see I want you all to myself?"

"I understand," Chloe said. "But I'm afraid Lilli doesn't. I have my worries about her that you don't, can't understand."

"I want to, though," Braden said. "I want to understand everything about you. But now let's just enjoy the rest of the evening—oh, yes, and eat. I'm starving. Okay?"

The restaurant was lit by candlelight with tables covered in white linen. The pasta and fish dinner they had was delicious. Braden was different tonight, more thoughtful than Chloe had ever seen him. Her disappointment with him vanished. She had never felt this close to him. They talked of childhood fantasies and fears, of schoolyard bullies, family idiosyncrasies and reoccurring dreams. This was Braden unwashed and rumpled and real and, because of that, lovable.

Later that evening, their kisses became long and tender, more satisfying and exciting than the night before. Both of them were content and relaxed now that the boundaries were in place, and their lovemaking turned into that, making love, not just being overwhelmed by passion.

As Braden was leaving, he said, "I've been debating all weekend whether you'd enjoy coming to Chicago for one of my parents' parties next Saturday night. But you have to meet them, Chloe. I want them to get to know you and love you as soon as possible. Will you come, for my sake? It would mean a lot to me."

Chloe hesitated. "But how would I get to Chicago and back from here?"

"I have a friend who has a small plane. Don't worry. He's an excellent pilot. If you can drive to the airport in Ludington, he'll take you to a small landing strip near my folks' home in the outskirts of Chicago, where I'll pick you up; and vice versa on the way back. Actually, I phoned him last night and made the arrangements. So you can see you'll have to go, if only to save me from looking like a fool."

"But, Braden, I have nothing suitable to wear," Chloe hedged.

"I trust your taste. But leave me out of the women's clothing arena. I'm no expert there, I'll admit. Say you'll go, Chloe. It will mean so much to me to have you there."

Chloe sighed. "Well, I'll certainly be out of my element. But I'll come."

"You're wonderful," Braden exclaimed, cupping her face in his hands and looking at her as though memorizing her features. "I'll miss you this week. I'll call you with more details. See you then." And with one last kiss, he was gone.

Monday Chloe and Lilli shopped for school clothes and for a dress for Chloe to wear next weekend. Her clients in Pentwater, about to close their pricey little shops for the season, were delighted to help her. They came home with four tops and three pairs of jeans for Lilli and a lovely shiny, floor-length black dress with black pumps for Chloe that she was assured would fit right in with Chicago society people. Lilli loved clothes, and the choice of hers and helping Chloe brought her much joy. Lilli excitedly showed Pops their purchases, which he admired for Lilli's sake.

But Pops wasn't happy with her trip to Chicago. Later that evening, when Lilli was in bed, he turned from the TV and said, "So this pretty boy is going to introduce you to his la-di-dah parents? And how am I supposed to manage on Labor Day weekend without you?"

"I'll make sure the rooms are ready before I go and help you reorganize when everyone leaves. Pops, you can handle it with Charlie, Maude and the maids, like you've always done. That's not the problem, and you know it."

Pops said with a grumble, "I just hate to see you get involved with someone you hardly know."

"I'm 27, Pops. And I'm getting to know Braden. And the only way I can get to know him is to have him come here or go to Chicago, since he lives there, right?"

Chloe took a deep breath. Something else had to be said.

"And, while you're upset anyway, I've been doing a lot of thinking lately—about Lilli, I mean."

"What about Lilli?" Pops asked, his face softening at the mention of her name.

"I think we should let David know Lilli is his

daughter."

Pops hung his head. Then, to Chloe's surprise, he said, "I know it. I've been thinking the same thing for some time." He looked up at Chloe. "We owe it to Lilli, don't we? She's more important than any promise we made to .... Marie ... her mother." Saying Marie's name brought tears to Pops' eyes. Chloe put her arms around him.

"It's time. It's time."

"It's so hard to let her go," Pops said, his voice quavering.

"With your permission, I'm going to tell Braden about it."

"Why bring him into it?"

"Why not? I don't feel like lying any more—to anyone—and especially to Lilli."

"I don't want Lilli hurt," Pops said emphatically. "We're not even sure David wants anything to do with her."

"Of course not. I'll tell Braden in strict confidence. Lilli should know nothing unless David wants to see her or acknowledge her. It would break my heart to see her harmed in any way by this."

"I know, Chloe," Pops said. "I know you love her like I do. We've been trying to protect her. But maybe we've been going about it in the wrong way."

"I'm hoping that Braden, by living in Chicago, may have heard about David or know how to locate him."

"Unless he's moved. Who knows?" Pops sighed. He patted Chloe on the shoulder. "But go ahead. Tell him. You have my permission."

"Jack is going to be at the airport Friday at 5:00," Braden said when he called later that evening. "He'll check in at the desk so you can make contact. Be on time, Chloe. He's a great friend to do this."

"Now you're making me feel guilty."

"Please don't. He knows all about you, how important

29

you are to me. You don't realize all the warnings I've given *him*. He has strict instructions not to crash while you're on board."

"That's reassuring," Chloe said with a laugh. Then she paused. "Braden, can I tell you something in confidence?"

"Of course." Braden sounded worried. "Is there a problem?"

"Nothing to do with you, with us," Chloe reassured him. "It's about Lilli."

"Lilli?"

"I haven't been totally honest with you about Lilli's situation. Actually, it's a family secret, one my sister Marie requested before she died. And I have to ask you to keep this in strict confidence."

"You can count on me."

"I know I can," Chloe said warmly. "You see, in fact, Lilli's father was never told of Lilli's existence."

"Why?"

"Marie didn't want to ruin David's marriage or cause him pain. But I think, for Lilli's sake as well as his, he should be told the truth at this point."

"It seems like the compassionate thing to do," Braden agreed. "But what if he wants nothing to do with her?"

"That's why we still need to keep it a secret, perhaps forever, unless he wants her in his life in some way."

"Thank you for trusting me with this, Chloe. How can I help?"

"Well, you live in Chicago. Maybe, if he still lives there, you could look him up. His name is David Trassault."

"David Trassault? I know of him. Didn't he have a show six months ago? Wait. I have an idea. I have a friend who owns a detective agency, and he owes me one. Because this David Trassault is so well known, it should be simple for him to track him down. I'll call him tomorrow."

"Thank you, Braden. A weight has been lifted off of

me."

"Anything to help my lady."

"You're sweet."

"I know. And I can't wait to see you. My parents are going to love you."

However, when the weekend was over, Chloe had no reason to believe that Braden's parents felt anything close to love for her.

5 MARK

Braden's parents' house was a huge white mansion with a long winding driveway, more grandiose than Chloe imagined. Braden was boyish and charming in his excitement, showing her places where he had fished as a child, trees he had fallen from. But meeting his parents was like taking a cold shower. They were well-dressed and haughty. Chloe saw his mother give her a cool once-over.

How disappointed she must be with her son's choice, Chloe thought. Braden, however, didn't appear to notice. *That or he's used to them,* Chloe thought. For all his eagerness to have her meet them, he seemed rather dismissive of his parents, pausing only for a brief introduction before showing Chloe the house and the room she was to stay in. Chloe noticed how formal and stiff they were with each other: mother, father, son. *What a thrill, turned out to impress people each day,* Chloe thought disdainfully.

If she had been 18, *she* might have been impressed. But at 27 Chloe had distinct opinions, and she found this "prestige" boring.

When alone at last in her beautifully furnished large room, she went to the open window to catch the breeze and let it filter through her hair.

"It's going to be a long weekend," Chloe murmured.

But breakfast the next morning was delicious. It was fun to be served. She and Braden spent the whole day roaming the grounds and rode some very spirited horses, too spirited for Chloe. Braden, on the other hand, was an excellent horseman.

As she awkwardly fell into Braden's arms after enduring a rousing gallop, Chloe exclaimed, "How am I going to manage in my heels tonight with these stiff, sore legs?"

Braden laughed. "Not much of a horsewoman, are you?"

"I survived," Chloe said, smiling grimly. "But if I get much stiffer, you're going to have to carry me around the dance floor."

The party was the gala chore Chloe had expected, with tuxes and long red fingernails and sleek hairdos. *I can see why Braden found me different*, Chloe thought. The appetizer tray was delicious and dinner divine. This almost made up for the dinner guests, who appeared made of cardboard. *Cookie-cutter women indeed*, Chloe thought. *Braden was right.*

Braden's parents introduced Chloe as Braden's business associate, which, of course, she was in a way. But it avoided the real issue.

Perhaps at 32 they're so used to Braden being single they can't believe he is serious about a woman, Chloe thought. *And there's little doubt they hoped for a more "socially acceptable person" than me.*

However odd this appeared to Chloe, Braden seemed happy, squeezing her hand as though she was the superstar of the party.

Men are so dense, Chloe thought. *Or maybe his parents always act this way.*

"I told you my parents would love you," Braden said at the end of the evening.

"They were very ... kind," Chloe said hesitantly.

But apart from the intense exhilaration and delight she was experiencing around Braden these days, Chloe breathed a sigh of relief as she drove her little green Mazda away from the airport and home again.

The next day Braden called, disappointment edging his voice. His father was sending him to California to assist in the renovation of a new acquisition there.

"Five weeks, Chloe. How will I stand it?"

Chloe wondered if this was his parents' reaction to her. But, again, it could be just business. Braden had told her before he was always traveling. She knew she would miss him; his touch, his actual physical presence.

"I'll call you in the morning and at night. So behave yourself," he said.

"No problem," Chloe responded. "This is Pentwater, remember?"

In the days that followed, Chloe's world seemed divided. When she talked to Braden, she became lost in his feelings and ideas. The sound of his voice was stimulating. She could still visualize him clearly. Chloe was beginning to feel a permanence in their relationship, a stability, though she had misgivings, especially where church and Lilli were concerned. He promised to make inquiries about David on his return to Chicago. Chloe was relieved she had told him. She knew he would find David.

They were fairly full at Manitou Inn in the early fall, mostly the over-60 set enjoying peace after the summer crowds. Lilli was ensconced and happy in 3rd grade. She liked her teacher, a sweet younger woman. Surprisingly, Lilli was annoyed with the art lessons at school. Her creativity rebelled at the simple projects the art teacher required. But all in all, things were going well. Chloe busied herself providing end-of-season sales figures for the stores in Pentwater she serviced, as well as helping Pops with his duties and seeing that the workmen, who were busy renovating Manitou Inn one room at a time, didn't disturb the guests.

I am happy here, Chloe thought. *I can see myself living alone, running the hotel—or trying to at least—at Pops' age.*

She started thinking about sharing a life with Braden, but the picture was fuzzy. She couldn't see living with him every day. He was a once-in-a-lifetime experience, she thought, or a few-month wonder. But then all her previous relationships had ended that way. What was wrong with her? Was she afraid of commitment because of what happened to Marie? Or was it because she couldn't picture leaving Pentwater for Chicago? She knew Braden would never live in Pentwater.

It was late September, the second weekend after her trip to Chicago, when clumps of red and yellow leaves amongst the green of the trees signaled the presence of fall and the air was cool. As Chloe walked into church with her father and Lilli, someone tapped on her shoulder. Chloe spun around to face Mark Lockley, remarkably unchanged, with a sheepish smile on his face.

"Hello, Chloe."

"Mark," Chloe burst out, unable to hide her surprise. "What are *you* doing here?"

"Going to church," he said, giving her one of those little twinkling smiles she remembered so well.

"I mean ..." Chloe stammered. "It's been so long."

"Years," Mark agreed with a sigh.

Lilli was pulling on Chloe's hand and led Chloe to their "favorite" pew next to Pops. Chloe watched Mark slide into a pew with his parents, just two pews in front of theirs.

The sermon was on forgiveness. Chloe struggled to listen, while all the time supremely aware of Mark sitting just two rows ahead of her with his dark curly hair and broad shoulders.

At coffee time Mark was surrounded by parishioners and his parents. He was, again, the focal point of Chloe's attention, though she tried not to look his way. There wasn't a person in church who didn't know about she and Mark; most had known them as children. So Chloe felt self-conscious approaching him, though she was dying to talk to him before he disappeared for years again.

Out of the corner of her eye, she saw him break away from the people surrounding him and his parents and walk in her direction. She rattled on to a woman about teaching kid's church next Sunday until she felt a hand cup her elbow. It was Mark.

"How nice of you to come to visit your parents," she began. "They're so proud of you."

Mark chuckled. "They might have got more than they bargained for. You see, I'm living with my parents for now until I can find a place of my own."

"In Pentwater?" Chloe stammered. "But I thought you lived in Detroit."

"Did," Mark said briskly. "I got a job at Dow Chemical in Ludington as an engineer. But I'll be living in Pentwater."

"Here?" Chloe repeated incredulously.

Mark burst out laughing. "Sure, here. I've lived here most of my life. *You* live here. 'Here' is good."

"Well, *I* think so," Chloe said slowly. "But ... will your wife join you here?"

Mark's face clouded. He looked down. "I'm freshly divorced. My former wife lives in Detroit."

As Chloe was digesting this, Mark brought out hesitantly, "Would you have dinner with me tomorrow night, Chloe, just to remember old times and catch up on each other?"

Chloe found herself nodding in assent, her mind churning.

"See you at 6:00 p.m. tomorrow, then. I'll pick you

up," Mark said, turning to talk to another church member.

When they got home from church, Chloe rushed upstairs to her room. She needed to be alone. She didn't want Pops or Lilli to see her so agitated.

Mark divorced and back in town to stay, she thought. *I can't believe it. This is the first time I've seen him since he left for college.* She had to admit she had secretly yearned for such a homecoming for years.

Not divorced, though, she thought. In fact, it was the news of Mark's marriage that ended all hope of his returning to Pentwater and, in fact, any hope at all.

When Braden called that evening, Chloe had a hard time focusing on what he was saying. But she hid her distraction well enough so that Braden was unaware of it.

Until I have myself under control, she thought, *I don't want to talk to Braden about Mark returning to Pentwater.* She didn't tell Braden she meant to see Mark the next evening. *What purpose would it serve?* she thought. *Mark is simply an old friend.* If this were true, though, why was Chloe in such a state she could barely put one foot in front of the other?

That night Chloe had trouble falling asleep and, when she did, she dreamed of Mark, dreams she couldn't recall the next morning, though she bolted awake sweating and agitated.

On Monday evening, Mark and Chloe were seated at Harbor Light, a little restaurant in the center of town.

After they had ordered, Chloe began, "So how was work today?"

"Like any new job, it's confusing. But I'm slowly adjusting."

"I'll bet it feels weird to be back in Pentwater after all these years."

Mark grimaced. "Whoa, girl. It's been nine years, not

twenty."

"Almost a decade," Chloe said with a sigh. "And so much has happened since you left."

"You're right," Mark said. "And not all of it terrific." He cleared his throat. "I want you to know how sorry I am about Marie—and your Mom."

"Those were huge losses," Chloe said, averting her eyes from his face. "But we have Lilli."

"Marie's child. I saw her with you in church. She's so cute, dark like ..."

"... David," Chloe finished. "She's got his artistic nature. She's always drawing."

Mark looked uncomfortable. "I should have been there for you during that time. But things got so ... complicated."

"I know," Chloe said. She deftly steered the conversation to less serious subjects like mutual friends and escapades they had shared as children. They laughed and talked, and the dinner ended pleasantly enough.

As Mark dropped Chloe off, he asked if he could see her Wednesday, just two days away. Chloe found herself begging off—and for Friday and Saturday as well.

Mark looked hurt. "Well, I'll call you."

"Yes," Chloe said with a smile. "Call me."

When the door closed behind him and Chloe had gone to bed, emotions that lay in the back of her heart swirled through her, sweet memories of their youth together. But with them came thoughts of that painful summer of Marie and David, her and Mark's short-lived romance, their breakup and Mark's departure. Chloe discovered she was angry with Mark, an anger she hadn't recognized until now. Mark deserted her when she loved him and needed him most. Without a look back, he went off to a world she had no part in. He married. He only returned to Pentwater after all these years because his life and marriage had fallen apart.

What was she supposed to do? Pick up their relationship again as a friend—or more? In her heart, Chloe's anger burned against such an idea.

He can cool his heels, Chloe thought—of course, not to mention Braden. She was sure Braden would not be pleased. In fact, she probably shouldn't have gone out to dinner with Mark. *He* is *an old friend, but that excuse only goes so far.*

Safe in her bedroom, Chloe muttered, "Who does he think he is, bursting back into my life like this? Does he think I'm eternally desperate and available? Well, I won't be hanging onto him pathetically again, not in *this* life, anyway."

6 THE PAST AND PICTURES

When Braden called later that night, Chloe didn't mention seeing Mark at church or their dinner Monday evening. Her feelings were too confused to talk about it. But Braden had news.

"Guess what? I called my detective friend today. He found an address for David Trassault. He said David was his easiest find ever and lives in a townhouse in the 'artsy section' of Chicago—his words, not mine."

Braden was pleased with himself, Chloe could tell, for being so efficient. But her fingers trembled as she carefully wrote the address on a piece of paper. *Now Lilli's fate is in my hands, literally,* she thought with a flutter of her stomach. Everything became real with the address.

"Braden, I'm sorry. I've got to share this with my father before he goes to bed, or I won't be able to sleep tonight."

"Well, okay," Braden said, sounding crestfallen. "But how about lonesome *me* out here in California? Now you're going to hang up? Maybe I shouldn't have told you."

Chloe felt impatient with him. Couldn't he see how important and disturbing this was to her? But she gently tried to soothe him.

"We'll talk tomorrow night twice as long."

"Well, okay. I'll hold you to that."

"Thank you, Braden. What you did was *so important* to me. And I ... I love you," she blurted out.

"You know I love you, Chloe, so much."

She hung up the phone gently, wondering why she had said that when her emotions were in such a jumble lately.

It was because I knew that's what he wanted to hear, she admitted to herself with some shame.

She ran down the stairs with the paper in her hand, almost bumping into Pops as he made his way to bed.

"Pops, can we talk?" she said.

"Can it wait? I'm tired. Did you and Braden run out of things to say?"

"Pops," Chloe began with exasperation, "Braden got David's address."

That got Pops' attention. He looked around nervously. "Where's Lilli?"

"She's been in bed for an hour."

Pops put his finger to his lips. "Shh. Let's go to the kitchen and close the door."

"Okay," Chloe said. And as they sat down in the worn kitchen chairs, Pops took a deep breath.

"What are we going to do now, Chloe? I'm frightened. I almost wish we could tear that address up. I'm so afraid of losing Lilli."

"Well, we've waited this long," Chloe said. "And we'll still have to wait until we can prepare Lilli and decide how to approach David. He may be upset at being contacted at all. On the other hand, he has every reason to be angry that he was not told of Lilli's existence."

"Frankly, *I* would be," Pops said. "I keep thinking of you and how I'd feel if I wasn't told you were alive."

Chloe put her hand in Pops'.

"I always thought Marie's request was misguided," he continued, "though I'm sure she made it with the purest motives."

"I agree," Chloe said. "Her worry was disrupting David's marriage. But, in truth, by behaving that way, he disrupted his own marriage."

"Right," Pops agreed. "But I feel, when we've told him, we've opened a can of worms. He could insist on flying here and seeing Lilli immediately. He might," Pops added with a quiver in his voice, "take her from us."

"That's a horrible thought. But it's occurred to me many times too," Chloe said, sighing.

Pops wiped at the tears forming in his eyes. "That's the worst—and so possible. He has the right."

"I know. I know," Chloe said, putting her arm around Pops' shoulders, which had slumped noticeably.

"We have the idea," Pops said, his face creased with pain, "but look what it involves."

"But we *are* right. Something has to be done. Nobody said doing the right thing is easy. Look at Jesus' crucifixion."

"Well, we never told Lilli her father was dead, just that he had gone away," Pops said. "And she's never pushed us into a corner."

"She's sure to have more questions about it as she gets older," Chloe replied. "And now she'll know."

"But we can't just spring this on Lilli," Pops insisted.

"Oh, no," Chloe agreed. "We should probably start by mentioning her father more often. I have some pictures that Marie took of David. Maybe I can show her those."

"Yeah," Pops said. "A little more emphasis on the fact that she has a living, breathing father."

"But nothing to raise her hopes too much until we find out David's intentions towards her," Chloe added. "And, Pops, you know you and I have tried to give Lilli a good life. She's had stability and love, something I don't think David and his wife could have provided her at that time. There were just too many issues. Maybe there still are. We have to remember that, that we did the best we could under the circumstances."

"I just don't want to lose her," Pops said, his voice trembling. "I know I can't keep her any more with a lie. But I pray God every night that Lilli stays with us in Pentwater."

"I can't imagine her anywhere else," Chloe said. "But that's in God's hands, not ours."

When Chloe lay her head on the pillow that night, she felt her and Pops' discussion, though difficult, was starting to heal the hurts surrounding Lilli's birth, which all three of them—she, Pops and Lilli—needed to move on to a full, happy life.

As the week progressed, the thought of Mark being in town, though she hadn't seen or heard from him since Monday night, was working on Chloe. Whenever she walked through Pentwater, she was tense, as though he might appear around every corner. In truth, he was more likely working at his new job at Dow Chemical in Ludington, a slightly larger town close to Pentwater. It was an understatement to say that his sudden arrival disconcerted Chloe. She ceaselessly ran over in her mind the events of their relationship—and especially the summer of their romance—and found, as she had Monday night, an anger unknown to her before.

I've never forgotten Mark. He was always in the back of my mind. I was sad—I'll admit it—when he was just a memory. My heart accepted I would always love him. But now that he's back in Pentwater, living and breathing, a memory no longer, I'm angry with him for "deserting" me. I can't even figure myself out. Maybe it's because I was so hurt and that he was so important to me.

Chloe tried to push her feelings—and her anger—into the background. She concentrated on the renovation, running the hotel and her accounts. These things were pleasant, meaningful and stayed pretty much consistent, the soothing quality of sameness. And she tried to concentrate on Braden, which wasn't difficult as he sounded so lonesome and needy of her in California.

"I miss you so much," he said, "more than I thought. Three more weeks 'til I see you again, unless I can't stand it. Then I'll make a special trip back. But—I can't do that. They have me busy seven days a week."

"You're in California, though," Chloe reminded him. "That's nice."

"It's nothing to me," Braden said, "except for my job. I *do* love that. But that doesn't make up for my emotional side, not seeing you." He suddenly chuckled. "Before meeting you, I didn't know I *had* an emotional side."

"Oh, Braden," Chloe said, laughing out loud. "You're so funny."

"It would be funny if it wasn't true," Braden replied. "You've opened up my life, Chloe. You know that? I'm even looking at things differently by thinking of how *you* would see them."

"That could be dangerous," Chloe responded lightly. But, in fact, Braden's protestations of love warmed her and gave her ego a boost when she most needed it. And she cared about him, she told herself; she really did.

On Wednesday, Chloe decided it was time to approach Lilli with a picture of her father. She went to an old photo album she kept in her room and thumbed through the pictures. Marie and she had taken many pictures that summer: David doing a muscle pose with his children hanging onto each arm; a laughing group at a beach barbeque; Mark pulling Chloe by the arms, attempting to drag her into the waves. Tears sprang to Chloe's eyes. She carefully closed the book and laid it down. After a moment, she composed herself and picked a full-face close-up of David with his guitar, one Marie had no doubt taken.

When Lilli came home from school, she flung her books on the sofa and turned on the TV. Chloe sat next to her, with the picture in her pocket, and watched cartoons for awhile.

"Lilli, I've shown you pictures of your father before, haven't I?" Chloe said, not really knowing how to begin.

"Hmmmm," Lilli mumbled, not taking her eyes from the screen.

"Well," Chloe continued hesitantly, "I found this one"—and she pulled the picture from her pocket— "while I was looking at my photo album. I thought you might want to see it."

Lilli glanced at the picture. "I've seen that one before. I've seen them all before, the ones you have in your room."

"You have?" Chloe said. "But not for a long time, though, right?"

Lilli looked at Chloe out of the corner of her eyes.

"Promise you won't be mad?"

"Oh, of course not, honey."

"Well..." said Lilli, a tear trickling down her cheek, "you might be when I tell you. I've been bad."

"Bad?" Chloe said. "How could you be bad, Lilli?"

Lilli looked straight at Chloe, her brown eyes enormous.

"I snuck in your room and looked at your pictures." She gulped. "I even stole some."

Chloe sighed, relieved. "Oh, Lilli, you can look at those pictures and even take them whenever you want. They're yours too."

"Really?" Lilli asked.

"Really, sweetie, of course they are."

"Oh, Chloe, I'm glad. Come with me," Lilli said, jumping off the couch and grabbing Chloe's hands. "I want to show you something."

7 TRANSITIONS

Lilli half-dragged Chloe up the stairs to her bedroom. And in "the pink palace," as Pops called it, Lilli went straight to her bed, skimming her hand under the mattress until she carefully removed an envelope containing four pictures, which she showed Chloe. Two were of David and two of Marie.

"These were the ones I took."

"Oh, Lilli. Why shouldn't you have them? They're your mom and dad."

"But that's not all. Wait."

Lilli walked to the closet and pulled out a big portfolio they had bought her to keep her drawings in. She removed a large pencil sketch from the back and handed it to Chloe. It was a drawing of a man and a woman walking with a little girl between them. All three were hand-in-hand. As Chloe looked closer, she could see the faces were those of David, Marie and Lilli. They were realistic enough to send shivers down Chloe's spine. And in spite of herself, Chloe burst into tears.

"Chloe, what's wrong? I'm sorry," Lilli sobbed. "See, you think I'm bad too."

Chloe wrapped her arms around Lilli, wetting her head with her tears.

"No, no, honey. It's just that it's so *real*. It's such a

good sketch I can remember Marie and David, and it makes me cry."

"Because you miss them?" Lilli asked, still sniffling.

"Very much, honey, and because I wish that picture could come to life, just as you've drawn it."

"Me too, Chloe. I dream about it all the time."

"You do? Oh, honey, you've never told me that."

"I thought it was too weird."

"Well, dreams are always weird. But this one's a good one. That's for sure."

"But it will never come true."

"Don't say never, honey. Momma is with Jesus. But maybe Aunt Chloe and Grandpa could start looking for your dad."

"Doesn't my dad want to see me, Chloe? Doesn't he love me?"

"No, honey. It's not that way at all. Your dad was far away when you were born and doesn't know about you. But if we're lucky, maybe we can find him for you."

"Would you, Chloe?" Lilli asked, her eyes alight. "Then half my dream could come true."

Again, after Lilli had gone to bed, Chloe cornered Pops.

"Pops, you won't believe what just happened. I showed Lilli David's picture, and it started an avalanche. She has drawn this picture of she, David and Marie. Well, it's so lifelike ..."

"Show it to me when Lilli's at school," Pops interrupted. "I want to see it."

"And she has dreams about her dad all the time. Boy," Chloe said, "we were wrong about her not missing her parents. I think she misses them terribly."

"One would only expect it," Pops said with a sigh. "So what do we do now? Apparently Lilli is ready and waiting."

"I told her we'd look for David, that he didn't know where she was or that she even existed."

"Well, I only hope she won't be disappointed," Pops

murmured.

"All this time she's been thinking of Marie and David," Chloe said. "And the sad thing is we didn't even know."

"Well, then it's on to David. And how do we approach him?"

"My thought is a letter. Tons of things I want to say to him are coming to mind," Chloe said. "And when I've written it, I'll show it to you for your approval."

"I can't think of a better way," Pops agreed. "So I guess you should start writing the letter."

"Pray that I'll find the right words."

Chloe couldn't wait to tell Braden about Lilli that night but, when she did, he was noncommittal, trying to turn the conversation to his thoughts about his job or his missing her. Chloe tried to excuse him because he had never had children, but she couldn't help resenting his disinterest. There always seemed to be a shadow when she talked to him about Lilli, almost as if he was competing with Lilli for Chloe's affection, which disturbed Chloe.

And then there was Mark. Chloe looked forward to seeing Mark in church the next Sunday. But when she did, he only said "hi" and made sure he was nowhere near her during coffee time. He seemed sullen and distant. It occurred to Chloe someone may have told him about Braden. In a small town like Pentwater, that kind of news travels like wildfire. And Mark's parents had seen Chloe with Braden that one Sunday in church. Freshly divorced men aren't usually too trusting of women. And she had rebuffed him after their dinner together with regard to seeing him again. Chloe couldn't resist glancing at him every now and then, just to reassure herself he was still there. Once in awhile she saw his gaze resting on her, though he quickly turned his head.

After church, when they were walking in the front

door, Pops sidelined sarcastically to Chloe, "Well, Chloe, now that Mark Lockley is back, you'll have two men on the string."

Without warning, Chloe exploded. "And what is wrong with that? I'm 27 years old. Do you expect me never to have male friends or never become involved with anyone? Do you want me to be a spinster to make up for Marie, for a mistake my sister made when she was 20?"

Pops looked appalled at her outburst. He quickly turned on his heels and stomped off. Luckily, Lilli hadn't come in yet. Chloe peered nervously out the window and saw her standing by the street doing a mutual cat hug with Melanie.

Oh, I'm so glad she didn't hear that, she thought. *But why does Pops always sneer at me about men?* Pops' attitude bothered her, not the remark itself, which was innocent enough. But she knew him. *We're the only adults left in our family. Though we get edgy with each other about running the Inn, we love each other like crazy. Is Pops worried I'll leave him as well as Lilli? I wish now I hadn't said anything. But he has to stop making those ridiculous statements.*

It occurred to Chloe that her own attitude had changed. Before she had been dismissive as well when Pops put down any relationship she had with a man. Now it was different. Now she cared. Was it Braden? Or perhaps even Mark's return made Chloe re-evaluate her own life and future.

Braden told Chloe Sunday night that, after he returned from California, he would be visiting Pentwater for at least five days, "to make up for lost time."

"I have to report back to my father about this hotel in California for a couple days to kind of get the data fed into the system, if you know what I mean. But by Thursday morning I'll be in Pentwater. And I'm not leaving until Monday or Tuesday."

"So about two and a half weeks," Chloe said.

"Not a day longer," Braden vowed. "This separation is driving me nuts."

"I'll be happy when you're here again," Chloe said truthfully. "Pops has a lot of questions to ask you, too many for me to mention over the phone."

"Yeah, that too," Braden said, sighing.

Chloe didn't tell Braden she was trying to compose a letter to David, one that was giving her a great deal of trouble. Sunday night, before he called, she sat down at the desk, pen and paper in hand, for about 30 minutes without a word going down on paper. Then, when the phone rang, she decided she must be too tired and gave up for the evening. Monday morning she did no better. It was hard to know where to begin. Even "Dear David" sounded odd to her, especially nine years after knowing him for one short summer. She did her accounts for awhile, ate lunch and decided to pick up some groceries in town.

It was a glorious September day. Pentwater was settling down nicely. There were no traffic jams and summer visitors, just warm "hellos" from people she had known all her life. Chloe breathed in deeply, loving the lake odor that came on the breeze. She turned the corner to head to the grocery store and nearly ran into Mark Lockley, who was heading in the opposite direction.

"Mark," she cried out with a sharp gasp. "Oh, you scared me."

"You'll never be safe in Pentwater again," Mark said, laughing outright at her shock.

"Aren't you supposed to be at work?"

"Well, I would be if I wasn't working second shift this week."

Chloe smiled. "Sorry. I guess that was nosey of me."

"Yeah. You were always that," Mark said with a chuckle.

Chloe hit his shoulder lightly. Suddenly it felt like he had never left, with his easy banter. How she had missed him. She gulped and fingered her shopping list.

"Heading to the grocery store?"

"Just for a few things."

"Mind if I join you?"

"As long as you don't expect me to buy you a treat."

"Just a small one."

Chloe laughed. "Fat chance."

She did buy him a candy bar, however, since he promised to carry the grocery bags home for her.

After stopping at Manitou Inn and putting the perishable food in the refrigerator, Mark said, "How about a walk down the pier?"

"Okay. Let me get my sweater. It's always breezy on the pier."

Pops came in the kitchen just then and shook Mark's hand. The men talked for a minute about how bad the fishing had been in Pentwater the last few years. Then Chloe and Mark left.

"I hear you've got a male friend," Mark said, not missing a beat.

"Yes, I do," Chloe replied with a smile.

"I hear he's from Chicago and his company is the one that's going to help your dad renovate Manitou Inn."

"That's right."

"I imagine you don't suffer from a lack of men in your life; am I right?"

"Oh, the line forms to the left."

"Well, you know what I mean."

"I've had my share, I guess."

"But you've never found someone you wanted to settle down with?"

"Not yet," Chloe said, deftly redirecting the subject, "not like you."

"Yeah. Not a very good idea, as it turned out." Mark sighed. "But it was good in the beginning. In college everything was so interesting, so ... happening. I loved my engineering studies. I wanted to get out of Pentwater, to get my first taste of the 'real world.'" He gave Chloe a quick look, as though realizing his comments might be painful to her.

They did open the wound, though she had guessed as much before. Chloe felt a deep aching anger in the pit of her stomach. But her pride forced her to remain calm. Mark must never guess how his leaving hurt her.

Reassured by her steady interest, Mark continued, "I met Susan then. She was part of my exciting new life, different and ... worldly and all. She seemed to have lived more, experienced more, growing up in Detroit."

Chloe managed to nod her head understandingly.

"We were together for my four years in college and got along great. So it seemed natural, after college, to get married and move to Detroit. Her father helped get me a job in a firm that his company did business with. But as soon as we settled into an everyday routine, things began to fall apart. The city was dirty and packed with people. All Susan and her parents talked about was 'getting ahead,' whatever that means. Material things were everything to them. Susan talked about her 'goals' for us. But it was never about our marriage; just a new house in a certain neighborhood, a particular type of car. It got boring. And she refused to go to church with me. I hadn't gone to church much in college, but I needed to then. So I ended up going alone. And I'm sorry to say, instead of thanking and praising God for his gifts to me, much of my prayer involved complaining about my disintegrating marriage and unhappiness with the way my life was going. I guess I was praying for a miracle, a way out of my current lifestyle."

"Well, I doubt you'd call this a miracle. But one night I discovered a letter from a male acquaintance of ours to Susan. It was obvious they were lovers. When I confronted Susan, she was unconcerned. She said she had intended to divorce me for some time and asked me to leave then and there."

"I was shocked. For all my unhappiness with my marriage, I assumed Susan and I would work it out. I stayed in a hotel for a few nights and then rented a studio apartment, waiting for the divorce to become final. I was miserable. But one thing soon became clear to me. I wanted to come home, back to Pentwater. I asked my parents to check around because employment is so limited here. After a couple of months, they told me they had read in the Ludington paper that Dow Chemical was hiring engineers. I interviewed and got the job. And here I am."

"Are you happy to be here, though, after being gone for so long?"

"Number one, it wasn't *that* long and, number two, the answer is 'yes.' You know what I wish? I wish I had returned to Pentwater right after college. I could have saved myself a lot of pain."

They were walking down the pier now, which was deserted save for a few fishermen waiting for a run of lake perch. Chloe, pondering on what Mark had said, glanced in their buckets—none yet.

"Unlike you," Chloe said slowly, carefully choosing her words, "I've never wanted to leave Pentwater."

There was a silence between them. Chloe looked at the lake. The waves were picking up, sending water splashing over the pier and leaving puddles as they retreated again.

"At least you can breathe here," Mark said with a sigh. "There's some tranquility."

That night, after talking to Braden, Chloe thought about Mark and their talk. She couldn't help feeling angry and hurt when Mark mentioned loving college and having fun with Susan, his future wife. Those were the worst years for Chloe, Marie's pregnancy and death, struggling to help Mom and Pops raise Lilli and then Mom's death. Chloe had to grow up fast during that time, while Mark had partied and loved someone else, barely giving her a thought. That hurt, because she *had* thought about him, thought about him a lot.

But he had suffered too, through his marriage and divorce. They had lived different lives for so many years. Yet she still felt close to him.

Chloe decided against telling Braden that Mark was back in town. Braden would know when he returned from California and maybe, if she was lucky, not even then. Chloe didn't want to make Mark an issue Her contact with him was innocent enough to be ignored.

8 THE LETTER

The next morning, Tuesday, after Chloe saw Lilli off to school and helped with departing guests, she told Pops she needed to work on the letter to David for at least a couple of hours in her room. This time she was determined to get *something* down on paper, no matter what.

She sat down at the desk and picked up the pen with determination. *Help me, God, get this thing rolling.* Now "Dear David" was on paper. With intense concentration, many rewrites and even some tears, Chloe surprised herself. The letter was done in less than two hours. She found Pops finishing a sandwich in the kitchen and stuck her finished draft under his nose.

"Well, let's see what it says," Pops said. He read aloud:

"Dear David: This is Chloe Henning. I'm writing on behalf of a lovely little girl who you have never met—Lilli, your daughter. She is now 8 years old and has seen pictures of you. She has been told you are far away and don't know about her, which, until this time, has been true. Her mother, my sister Marie, made our family promise not to tell you, David, about your daughter because she was afraid it might disrupt your life, your marriage. But Marie has been dead many years now—she died soon after Lilli was born—and Pops and I feel you should know about Lilli. I realize what a shock this must be to you, David. In my heart, I hope you remember the events of that summer nine years ago. But she *is* your daughter, David. She is also all we have left of Marie, and we love her so. This letter is an attempt to give Lilli back at least one of what she wants and needs so badly—her own parents.

I'm well aware how disruptive this letter could be to your life, and the pain it could cause you. That's why I am sending it confidentially to you alone at your office. It is intended for your eyes only. At our end, we have not told Lilli you are actually pretty near, in Chicago. We have only said we would try to find you. If you wish it, all communication can end with this letter. We will simply tell Lilli we could not locate you.

In fact, everything from this point on is up to you. We don't want to lose Lilli, of course. She has been our delight these eight years, and you can rest assured she is happy and safe.

We will await your response. And if you choose to send no response—well, that is a response in itself. God bless you, David, you have created a wonderful little girl. Chloe Henning, Manitou Inn, Pentwater, Michigan."

Pops brushed at his eyes. "That's absolutely wonderful, Chloe. I wouldn't change a word."

"I think God gave me inspiration, because I've never written such a difficult letter."

Pops cleared his throat, trying, Chloe saw, not to cry.

"I hope it's not the beginning of losing our darling."

Chloe patted his gnarled hand on the kitchen table.

"I remember David as a warm, sensitive, joyous individual," she said. "Let's believe he'll respond the right way."

"Which is?" Pops said with a sigh.

"I don't know," Chloe said frankly. "We'll just have to wait and see, I guess. But don't you feel relieved we're finally doing the right thing for Lilli?"

"I hope it's the right thing," Pops said quietly, staring out the kitchen window.

"We'll just have to trust God," Chloe said. "But I know now we've done what we should have done a long time ago."

Pops sat down, holding his head in his hands. He looked up at Chloe. "When are you going to mail it?"

"Well, I'm going to wait a couple days and just look at it a bit. I guess I'm in shock. In a way I can't believe we're doing this."

"I can't either," Pops replied.

"Why don't we say by the end of this weekend, at the outside only five days, it will be in the mail? And if you want to reread it during that time, feel free, Pops. We have to make sure we've said what we want to say the way we want to say it."

"Because once it's in the mail," Pops said, finishing her thought, "it's gone forever."

"Exactly."

It was Sunday morning, before church, when Chloe looked the letter over again, as she had countless times during the last few days. Her mind, however, had become blank and frozen. Once the words went down on paper, they turned to stone. And try as she might, she could not change them for the better. *I'm so scared. But this has to go in the mail tonight, or I'll lose my nerve.* She looked at a picture of Lilli when she was 3 years old that sat on her dresser. *I just can't lose her. Oh, God, please don't let me lose her.* With that, she dressed hurriedly, craving the peace she found in God's house.

This Sunday she was teaching kid's church. As she readied the craft materials she would use for the art project, she saw Mark, resplendent in a suit and tie, walk past the classroom door and wave. *Why is he so dressed up?* she thought. Then she remembered a conversation she had last week with Mrs. Ryman, an older woman in her church.

"That Mark Lockley, he offers to usher as soon as he's back in town. Isn't that fine?"

Chloe smiled. Mrs. Ryman always thought the best of people.

"And he's volunteered to lead the youth group too. I suppose you've heard of his divorce. That poor boy. They say his wife was horrible to him. We're lucky to have him back in Pentwater, don't you think, Chloe?"

Chloe nodded absently. Actually, at that time she had been glancing about, trying to catch a glimpse of Mark herself. But now Mrs. Ryman's words came back to her.

Kids Church went well that morning. Lilli helped Chloe by passing out materials and carefully supervising the craft project. *She looks like a little mother*, Chloe thought fondly. *Nobody is better with 3-year-olds than an 8-year-old. They're just old enough to be a real help and yet young enough to understand where the little ones are coming from.*

After church she was just putting the craft materials away and rearranging the desks when Mark poked his head in the door.

"Need any help?"

"Sure," Chloe said. "By the way, I can't tell you how few times I've seen you in full regalia, a suit and tie. You look good."

Mark beamed. "Well, when you knew me best, I was a kid. Actually, this is my outfit more often now, more often than I'd like, actually."

"And I hear you're leading the youth group now."

"Well, I get sick of sitting in front of TV nights at my parents' home. So it will get me out. And the kids are great. I think I'll get more out of it than they will."

"Lilli's in that group."

"I know," Mark said softly. "Our first meeting is next Wednesday. Why don't you come too?"

"I ..." Chloe began, but was interrupted by someone

calling "Mark" from the door. Chloe turned around to see Marcie Turner, a young woman who had graduated from high school a year behind Chloe and Mark. She still lived with her parents on a farm outside of town and worked in the library in Ludington. Chloe noticed that Marcie was dressed to the hilt today in a flowered dress with her dark hair pulled back and curled.

With a nod to Chloe, Marcie said, "Mark, come with me. There are some people at church today you haven't seen in ages."

Mark rolled his eyes at Chloe when Marcie's back was turned, but meekly followed her.

At the door, Marcie looked back at Chloe and said, "I'm helping Mark lead the Youth Group. So you really don't need to come Wednesday night."

Mark stopped, saying pointedly with a stubborn look, "Please come on Wednesday, Chloe. *I* would like you to. And I'm sure Lilli would appreciate you being there for the first meeting."

"I'll be sure to come," Chloe said with a smile, enjoying Marcie's discomfiture.

But when she got home from church, Chloe felt blue. Gathering up Lilli and, yes, Melanie, the three made their way to the beach to make sand castles. Since it was a mild day in late September, they dressed in sweatshirts and shorts. After helping the girls dig a channel to the lake, make a moat and form the foundation walls of a castle, Chloe sat on a beach towel. Lilli and Melanie made sand stalagmites on the castle by running the watery sand through their fingers.

As she watched them dreamily, they began whispering to each other, breaking it off in giggles.

"What's so funny, honey bunch?" Chloe asked Lilli.

"You know that Mark?"

"Mark Lockley? Sure. I told you I went to school with him."

"Well, he told me to make sure you came to our youth

meeting Wednesday and ..." Here again Lilli and Melanie exploded into more torrents of giggles.

"And?" Chloe said, waiting a little impatiently for their hilarity to end.

"And Melanie heard her mother talking on the phone and ..." Lilli stopped with dramatic flair.

"Go on, Lilli."

"... she told somebody that you and Mark were sure to get married now that he was back in town and 'free,' whatever that means."

"Was Mark in prison, Chloe?" Melanie asked.

Chloe had to smile. "The answers to your questions are 'no' and 'no.' No, Melanie, Mark was never in prison. 'Free' means he's ... no longer married."

"Oh, I'm glad," Melanie said, sighing. "I'm glad he wasn't in jail."

"*Could* you marry Mark, Chloe?" Lilli asked.

"Could but won't," Chloe said.

"Why not?" Lilli asked, a frown creasing her brow. "He's nicer than that Braden."

"You just don't know Braden very well, honey."

"Braden never listens to what I say," Lilli said, "but Mark does."

"We like him," Melanie added.

Chloe laughed. "Well, Mark will be glad to know he has the seal of approval from the young women in town."

"I just said he's nice," Lilli said with a disgusted look. "*I* don't want to marry him."

"But we think *you* should," Melanie said. Then the girls, aware of their boldness, deserted the sand castle gleefully and ran headlong down the beach away from Chloe. They ran so fast and so far it took Chloe a half hour to catch up to them. All three of them were exhausted by the time they made it back to Manitou Inn.

As they came in the door, Chloe looked at the cubby hole by the entryway. The letter was there. Pops had apparently read it, sealed it and stamped it. All Chloe had to do was mail it. And now he was waiting for them.

"I'll be right back," Chloe said, picking up the letter.

Pops put his finger to his lips, nodding towards Lilli, who had plopped down in front of TV and was watching cartoons. Pops had a fear of Lilli realizing the letter was going to her father. To Chloe, Lilli seemed oblivious in regards to such things as letters coming and going. *But, then again, I didn't know she was drawing pictures of David and Marie either*, Chloe thought.

Chloe walked slowly toward the mailbox at the end of the block. Autumn was moving along rapidly. Each day, more bushes and maple trees burst into flaming oranges, yellows and reds. A leaf brushed Chloe's cheek and she caught it, turning it over in her hand. It was life's cycle—the aliveness of summer, the dying of autumn, the stillness of winter and the rebirth in spring—each season a miracle and lovely in its own way.

Quickly and with trembling hands, Chloe slipped the letter into the mailbox and felt the door bang shut. Her body felt clammy and sweaty at the same time. *The thing that worries me most*, Chloe thought, *is that Pops and I have no legal claim on Lilli, not like David has. We're putting Lilli's destiny into the hands of a man we hardly know.* But the letter was mailed. It was over. *Now whatever happens happens*, Chloe thought, but the lingering fear stayed with her.

Later that evening, while Chloe tried to focus on Braden, who would be calling promptly at 9:00 o'clock, she couldn't help being distressed about Lilli and Mark. It felt like the people she loved were being pulled away from her. Though Mark didn't appear enamored with Marcie, with Braden coming gangbusters into Chloe's life, she knew Mark would turn to other women. And that thought bothered her more than it should.

I shouldn't care, not after all that's happened—or hasn't happened, I mean—between us, Chloe thought. *Mark chose another life and left me behind. Is that the kind of man I want, one who deserted me without a care? Braden has been decisive and positive from the beginning. Braden is sure he wants me in his life, even if sometimes I'm not sure I want to be in his—forever, that is.*

It was 9:00 o'clock, and the phone began ringing. She picked up the phone and could almost visualize Braden; his face, his hair, his love of her. The feeling was almost palpable in the gloom of this evening.

"Oh, Braden, I mailed the letter to David today," Chloe said, and promptly burst into tears.

"Don't worry, Chloe. It will turn out fine. You did the right thing. I'm proud of you."

"Oh, I just don't know," Chloe said, sobbing. "I'm so afraid he'll just ... take her."

"I'll make sure he doesn't," Braden said staunchly. "Our company works with a top attorney firm. David abandoned Marie and, by doing that, he abandoned Lilli as well. He can't come back and take her away from you now."

Chloe wasn't sure about the legality of this. But Braden's firmness comforted her. She could feel his arms around her, steadying her. They talked a long time, and Braden soothed Chloe into a more reasonable state of mind. When Chloe hung up the phone that Sunday evening, she realized Braden's call had been the brightest spot of her day.

9 FISHING WITH MARK

"Chloe, you promised to come to the youth meeting on Wednesday," Lilli reminded her at dinner on Tuesday. "We're going to have a fall festival party at church this year instead of going trick or treating."

"Does that bother you?" Chloe asked doubtfully.

"No," Lilli said with a firm shake of her head. "It will be better. We're going to have cider and donuts at church in our Halloween costumes and then go for a hayride at Marcie's farm. We get to see farm animals, like cows, pigs and horses."

"Have you decided what you want to be this year?"

"Yes," Lilli said. "Either a ballerina or a princess."

Chloe stifled a grin. Lilli always wanted feminine outfits at Halloween. Chloe remembered *she* was quite different. She loved to dress as a ghost, a witch, a hobo—not Lilli. It was frills, not chills, for her.

"I've made some sketches," Lilli said, putting a sheath of papers on the table.

Chloe looked through them with apparent seriousness.

"Well," she said, "I guess it's time to get the clothes box out." The clothes box contained clothing remnants and parts of former Halloween costumes, which Chloe and Lilli would use to form this year's costume. Chloe would pull out the old sewing machine and, following Lilli's drawings, the costumes turned out surprisingly well.

Pops was always amazed and proud of them both. And, besides this, Lilli was learning the basics of sewing, which she loved.

"C'mon, Chloe," Lilli said, pulling at her hand. They found the box in the attic and spent two hours sorting, cutting and basting. At the end of that time, it was clear Lilli would make a lovely ballerina after adding some dramatic dashes to one of her dance class ensembles.

The first thing Chloe noticed on Wednesday night, as she and Lilli walked into the gathering hall at church, was Marcie talking to Mark up close and personal over in the corner while the children ran about. Seeing Chloe, Mark waved to her and Lilli. Then he began settling the children down to begin the meeting. Chloe couldn't help being impressed by how he handled them. He commanded the attention—well, almost all the time—of the most fidgety boys. He always had a pack of little girls hovering around him. Marcie explained what would happen on the farm, hayride rules and how to treat the animals. Then Mark helped them to plan the party, who should bring what food and ideas for costumes.

After the meeting, Mark separated himself from Marcie, who was offering him a ride home.

"Thanks, Marcie," he said. "But I'm going to see Lilli and Chloe to Manitou Inn and then walk home."

"But, Mark, you'll be tired out," Marcie protested.

"My parents live in Pentwater, remember? It's a ten-minute walk from Manitou Inn. I've walked it many times," he said, with a significant look at Chloe.

"Well, see you soon, Mark," Marcie said, giving up. "But, remember, you promised me we'd ride-share to Ludington tomorrow morning."

"I remember," Mark said, with a slight grimace.

As the three of them walked home in the moonlight, crunching the papery leaves under their feet, Mark said, "Well, where is this Braden I've been hearing about?"

"In California," Chloe said shortly.

"Seems he's been gone awhile. You'd think it would be hard to leave you for such a long time."

"He'll be here next Thursday," Chloe answered, suddenly wanting to hurt Mark. "He's coming as soon as he can. Don't worry. *He* won't be gone for years."

Mark didn't say anything for a couple minutes. But instead of being offended, he said, "If you two are free this weekend, would you like to see if the fish are biting on Bass Lake?"

"Fishing?" Lilli cried. "Yes, yes, yes, yes. *I'll* go."

"It's a package deal. Your Aunt Chloe has to come too."

Lilli wrapped her arms around Chloe's waist, lifted up her feet and hung on her, almost making Chloe lose her balance.

"Please, please, can we? Say 'yes.'"

Chloe disengaged Lilli's arms gently. "Oh, you know I'm a sucker for you," she said, laughing at Lilli's excitement. She turned to Mark. "What time?"

"Let's go early Saturday morning. If the sun rises too high, they won't bite. How about if I pick you two up at 6:00 o'clock?"

"Okay," Chloe said. "But you know what this means, Lilli—no overnights with Melanie Friday night."

"I know. I know," Lilli squealed happily, already planning how she would tell Melanie about fishing with Mark and how jealous Melanie would be.

While Lilli dashed in the front door to tell Pops, Mark put a hand on Chloe's arm.

"Hey, Chloe, talk to me a minute before you go in," he said.

Chloe softly closed the front door. They moved to a

swing off to one side of the porch.

Lilli peeked her head out. And Chloe firmly said, "Homework, Lilli. You've only got an hour before bed."

Lilli hesitated. But then Chloe heard Pops calling her from inside the house, and Lilli disappeared again.

They were silent awhile, silhouetted by a half moon among the shadowy trees surrounding the porch, making the porch swing creak as their bodies shifted against the stiff wood.

"Feels good to be home again," Mark said.

"I'm glad you are," Chloe responded truthfully.

"So, this Braden guy, you serious about him?"

Chloe thought for a moment.

"It's serious, I guess, more so than any relationship I've experienced lately. But I probably need more time to know Braden. We've not been together long."

"You're not engaged or anything?"

"Who's being snoopy now?" Chloe retorted, the darkness hiding her smile.

"Well, I've got to get this straight," Mark said. "I don't want a run-in with some large angry boyfriend."

"Don't worry. Braden is not a barbarian type," Chloe said, laughing. "But he could get jealous."

"Hmmm," Mark said thoughtfully. He stood up suddenly and offered his hand to Chloe, jostling the swing into more creaks and groans. After he helped her to her feet, they stood close to each other in the moonlight. Mark still held Chloe's hand. To Chloe, the touch of his palm was a warm glow drawing her in. Mark bent towards her.

"You're so beautiful," he murmured.

Just as his lips were about to touch hers, however, Chloe jumped back, dropping his hand.

Mark stood frozen, trying to catch her expression.

"I'm sorry," he brought out. "I shouldn't have."

"No, you shouldn't have," Chloe murmured.

"This won't jeopardize our fishing excursion Saturday, if I promise to behave?"

Mark sounded jaunty and friendly again. But Chloe's fear was not just of him behaving but herself as well.

"No. That's fine. We'll be ready," she said softly, backing towards the safety of the door.

"See you then," Mark said. And with a wave of his hand, he disappeared into the shadows.

Chloe was quiet when Braden called that evening.

"You seem preoccupied tonight. Anything the matter?"

"No," Chloe said. But, of course, that wasn't true. Chloe was confused and disconcerted over Mark's near-kiss. Her feelings for Mark, never dead, had sprung alive with his touch, and Chloe frankly didn't know what to do with them.

When Braden hung up, Chloe lay in bed and went through all she could remember about her and Mark's long friendship and short romance. Then Chloe thought about Braden. After what seemed like a long time, Chloe finally slept. But she had terrible dreams. She would be with Mark, and he would be kissing her. Then he would turn into Braden—or vice versa. Her dreams were permeated with anxiety about who she was *really* with. Then Lilli appeared, and she was crying. Even Marie was there, whispering to Chloe. Was she trying to warn her?

Chloe awoke in a sweat and was relieved to find herself alone in her peaceful room with the morning sunlight filtering through the curtains. Downstairs she could hear Pops telling Lilli to eat her breakfast or she would be late for school. Then she heard Lilli's steps on the stairs. *Oh, wonderful normalcy*, she thought, and quickly dressed to start the day.

Thursday and Friday Chloe did her accounting work quickly, painted a room, tried a new hamburger casserole, made brownies and helped Maude wash the curtains.

"Where did you get all this energy?" Pops asked in amazement Friday evening after eating the casserole and brownies. "Why couldn't I get you to work this way before?"

"Pops, you know I work hard," Chloe protested. "I just want to keep busy, is all."

"Busy? During the last two days, I'd call you frantic."

Chloe managed a smile. The truth was her mind was whirling and her emotions in an upheaval. The chores stabilized her. It also helped her sleep, because each night she was exhausted.

She called Braden at his hotel Friday night because she needed sleep and the fishing excursion with Mark would start at 6:30 a.m. Saturday morning. When he asked why she was calling so early, Chloe said she was tired without mentioning the fishing. Chloe felt guilty because she hadn't told Braden anything about Mark. She had a feeling he wouldn't be pleased. *I'll just wait until he gets here. There's no harm done*, she consoled herself, carefully avoiding the issue of how she felt about Mark.

Lilli had to be dragged out of bed Saturday morning before dawn, struggling into the warm layers of clothes Chloe insisted she wear, for this October morning in Pentwater was chilly. Chloe saw Mark pull up in his dad's old pickup hauling a wooden boat and motor that she remembered from her youth. Fishing poles dangled from the back of the boat. Lilli squeezed into the truck first and sat between Chloe and Mark.

Bass Lake was as smooth as glass as Mark eased the boat and trailer into the water. The stars were fading as the sky lightened to the east, and the moon became a mere outline. Chloe, nestled in the front of the boat, sighed and dipped her fingers into the cold, dark water while Mark attempted to show Lilli how to attach a worm to a hook. Lilli squealed when the dirt-covered worm was put in her hand, immediately dumped the worm on the bottom of the boat and let Mark bait her hook. Mark threw a worm to Chloe and Chloe calmly looped it onto her hook, to Lilli's amazement.

"Oh, Chloe, how can you stand that?"

"I'm used to it, dear."

"Your Aunt Chloe and I did a lot of fishing when we were younger." Mark said. "She was quite the fisherman."

"I always *did* come away with more fish than you, didn't I?" Chloe said, laughing.

"Well, I wouldn't say *that*," Mark replied with a snort. "I just said you were good; *I*, on the other hand, was *great*."

"Great at telling fish stories anyway," Chloe said with a guffaw.

"Don't believe a word your aunt says. Now I'm going to teach you how to catch the big ones."

The plastic bucket filled with water remained fishless for the first half hour, while the sun's rays slowly edged through the trees, giving the lake a brighter, if less mysterious, feel. Then one pole jerked, and another, as the fish began to nibble at the bait. One sleek, sharp-finned fish after another lay thrashing on the boat's bottom. Mark and Chloe struggled to keep up, carefully pulling the sharp prongs of the hook from the fish's mouth, tossing the small fish back with a slap into the water and throwing the bigger ones into the bucket.

Chloe gazed at the dark water with its swaying seaweed. This was a part of her youth she loved; the fishy odor on her hands, the boat bobbing on the water. Lilli had caught three fish. But as the strike of fish slowed, then stopped, her excitement turned to grogginess as the fresh air enveloped her. She fell asleep leaning against Mark's knees, her pole still dangling over the water. It didn't matter, as there would be few bites until evensong.

Chloe and Mark stared at Lilli and smiled knowingly at each other. They were quiet and heard a loon call and the twitter of awakening birds. Mark cast his line into the lake with a "plop" as Chloe languidly stirred the water with her hand, her pole across her knees. She couldn't remember being this happy or peaceful. It was as though, she thought, she had awakened from her nightmare of the past week to this pleasant dream. She didn't dare look at Mark. He would read too much in her eyes. In a soft trance, she stared at the ripples her hand made in the water.

After a few minutes, Mark whispered, "What are you thinking about?"

Chloe looked up as though startled. She smiled, waving her hand in a sweeping gesture.

"Oh, that all this is perfect, this moment."

"I feel the same way," Mark said, giving her a meaningful look.

Chloe dipped her head and smiled.

10 BRADEN RETURNS

Chloe had mixed feelings about Braden's return. He had flown from California to Chicago Sunday night and called Monday evening. He sounded excited, saying he would be working with his father on settling the deal on the new California hotel and would be driving up early Thursday morning. In a sense, she was anticipating his return with pleasure for, in the last couple weeks, Braden had become more serious, in an indescribable sort of way. And Chloe knew it was because of her.

"Guess what?" he had said Monday night. "I went shopping today, and I bought you something. What do you want?"

Chloe laughed. "Aren't you putting the cart before the horse? Aren't you supposed to ask me what I want *before* you shop?"

"No," Braden replied firmly. "Then you've lost the element of surprise."

"Okay. You've got that," Chloe retorted. "*I'm* just happy you bought me *something*. But now you've caught me empty-handed because I didn't think we were going to exchange gifts. I'm afraid I have nothing for you in return."

"Oh, yes," Braden said significantly. "I'm hoping to get *a lot* from you in return."

After that comment, their conversation turned to when he would arrive in Pentwater Thursday morning. But Chloe felt, as she hung up the phone, that whatever Braden had in store, it was meant to take their relationship to a new level. This gave Chloe butterflies in her stomach, a mixture of happy yet uneasy feelings. Chloe was getting to be an expert lately of "not thinking" about certain aspects of her life, like her feelings for Braden or Mark. Her father's comment about "two men on the string" was coming back to haunt her, especially now that Braden would be back in Pentwater.

How I wish I had Marie or Mom to talk to, Chloe thought with an ache in her heart. *Pops is irritating and totally worthless in this area. I need a woman's intuition.*

Then Chloe thought of someone she trusted and could *always* talk to. She dropped to her knees. Chloe was aware she had a prayer problem. It wasn't that she didn't pray. In fact, sometimes it felt as though she was *always* praying. But her prayers fell into two categories, neither traditional. One was a running daily "conversation" with God about immediate things: praise of a blue sky, worries about Lilli, hoping the "bump, bump" in her car didn't mean car trouble—everyday problems and joys. These were talks with her heavenly friend.

The other type of prayer came less often, was *always* in the privacy of her room and was much more distinct. Most of the time Chloe didn't even realize she was going to pray until her emotions overwhelmed her and she fell to her knees, sometimes even laying down on the floor. For whatever reason, Chloe found it necessary at these times to get as close to the ground as possible. And here she was.

"Dear God," she prayed, "I've gone for a long period with only Lilli and Pops to share my life with. And I've been happy. But now, in the space of a few weeks, two significant but very different men have entered my life. I should be grateful and happy—and I am—but also confused and worried. Will Braden learn to love you as I do? Will he love Lilli? Can I trust Mark after he left me once? Help me, Lord. Be with me as I try to figure my way to the future."

After laying quietly on the floor for awhile, Chloe stood up and immediately plopped into bed without washing her face or brushing her teeth. She turned out the light and lay in the darkness, letting her thoughts swirl around her like the nighttime breeze. She knew that Braden and Mark in Pentwater at the same time meant confronting her feelings, some of which she wasn't sure of yet. She would have to choose a direction to travel, and that direction would not include both men.

I'll listen to what my heart says and do a lot of praying, Chloe thought. But that thought did not bring the peace she was longing for. She spent the night tossing and turning with uneasy dreams, not sleeping much at all.

Braden had, somewhat dramatically, kept up a conversation with Chloe on his cell phone as he drove to Pentwater. So Chloe was ready and waiting on the sidewalk when his shiny red Jaguar appeared. Looking taller, tan and better looking than ever, Braden sprang from the car and took Chloe in his arms. After their long embrace ended, Chloe saw Lilli watching them soberly from the porch.

"What's the matter, sweetie?" Chloe asked sheepishly, walking hand-in-hand with Braden towards the house. Lilli, however, didn't answer and bolted down the steps towards the sidewalk. Chloe, worried, looked after her until she saw Melanie.

"Going to Melanie's, honey?"

"Yeah," Lilli called over her shoulder, and the two girls ran off.

After coming in the front door, Braden went up to Pops and shook his hand.

"Good to see you, sir," he said. "I hear you have some questions for me."

"I do," Pops said with a wicked grin. "And I hope you have some answers for me."

"How is the renovation going?"

"There have been some glitches. But overall I'd have to say I'm pleased. But then you should know this after talking with one member of our family nightly."

"Oh, Pops," Chloe said with a sigh. "Braden and I don't talk renovation."

"You don't?" Pops replied ironically.

"No, sir," Braden said, grinning broadly as he threw his arm around Chloe's shoulders in a newly proprietary manner. "I make it a point to keep my personal life separate from business."

"Well," Pops said with a gleam in his eye, "I hope you'll be combining the two since you'll be staying at Manitou Inn until Tuesday."

"No problem," Braden answered, instantly serious. "Have you got any pressing concerns for me?"

"No, no," Pops said, backing off. "You two can enjoy yourselves for today."

"I'll show Braden some stuff," Chloe said. "Okay, Pops?"

"Yeah, yeah," Pops grunted, leaving the room. "Good to see you again, Braden."

As soon as Pops left the room, Braden reached for Chloe and held her close.

"You can't believe how I've missed you," he whispered in her ear, sending a chill down Chloe's spine. Her body convulsed in a quick little shudder. Braden lifted her face to his kiss. His arm encircling her waist pulled her close. Though it was broad daylight and Pops or Lilli could come in the room any time, Chloe felt alone and drowning, engulfed in Braden's intense physical and emotional presence. Her eyes fluttered open to find him staring at her, even as they kissed. *How huge his eyes seem*, Chloe thought groggily. Though they remained tightly locked together for only a few seconds, it felt like forever. Something had changed, evolved in their relationship since Braden left for California, and Chloe instantly felt the force of it. Braden's emotions and needs, now that he was physically present, dominated her in a way she hadn't felt before or during their separation.

"Oh, honey," Braden whispered into her hair when they finally drew apart. "Six days isn't long enough. We have to be together all the time."

Chloe, pressed against his chest, found herself saying, "I know, I know." And suddenly she felt she *did* know, did realize that this tide of emotion must bind them together always. All her doubts were useless now, blown away by his passion for her and her reaction to it. Without warning, tears trickled down Chloe's cheek and wetted Braden's shirt.

"Why are you crying, sweetheart?"

"I don't know."

Braden's fingers tenderly brushed the tears from her face. "Don't worry, Chloe. I'll take care of you."

Chloe looked up at Braden. His eyes shone with tenderness. No one had ever said that to her, "I'll take care of you." But Braden standing before her, saying it and meaning it, made Chloe realize how much she wanted that, to be taken care of.

"Oh, Braden, you're so good to me," she said with sincerity.

"I love you, Chloe. You know that."

"Yes, I know," Chloe said softly.

"We're going to be so happy," he said significantly. Chloe supposed that they were. She felt like she had lost her own will and must follow Braden's lead.

By the next morning, Chloe found that whatever she did—tend to Lilli, work on her accounts or her hotel duties—would have to be done with Braden glued to her like wallpaper. Her only release was his hours with

Pops inspecting and supervising the renovation of Manitou Inn. Even Braden realized Pops turned belligerent and nothing was accomplished with Chloe present. Chloe wondered when Pops' antipathy towards any man she was interested in would end. But when Pops and Braden were alone together and doing what made them both happy, they were fine. Chloe could see how Braden loved his work.

Chloe found, with relief, that Braden was making attempts to win Lilli over, though he always insisted Chloe participate too. It was: "Lilli, show me your pictures. Wow, that's great. What do you think of that one, Chloe?"

But Chloe appreciated this effort, and it was apparent Lilli did too. She warmed up considerably to Braden and began to chatter freely with him. Braden even worked on a difficult "pizza" puzzle with Lilli and Melanie for a couple of hours one day, while Chloe read a book at his side. At these times Chloe, watching Lilli, could see how she craved a father figure in her life. This brought Chloe's thoughts back to that letter, which had by now found its way to Chicago and David. Not that she had forgotten. It was always on her mind. She rushed to get the mail every day and was half-ready for "that" phone call.

It's only been 12 days, Chloe thought. *I couldn't expect him to respond so soon. He needs time to absorb it.* But now he knew. That was a queer feeling. She knew it was eating at Pops too. However, with Braden there, he wouldn't discuss it.

How strange Braden staying at Manitou Inn was. Pops, with Chloe's total approval, gave him a room in the guest block far away from the family section of the house. But it was odd to watch TV late at night without Braden having to leave, as though they were married already. Braden hemmed and hawed when it came time to say good night. Chloe knew he would join her in her bedroom in an instant if she let him. Instead, her room was Chloe's sanctuary, a place of peace away from Braden's presence, which seemed to surround her more each day. Chloe hardly knew how she felt any more. But she knew she was moving towards Braden rapidly, a thought both delicious and frightening.

Braden controlled Chloe with his ardent love-making, the result of a long history with women and the uniqueness of his feelings towards her. She felt a joyful white heat in his arms and craved his touch, his kisses. He respected her boundaries, which left them necking like teenagers and only whetted their desire for each other. Chloe felt he would be an excellent lover and knew he loved her. But was this enough to base a life together on?

Unfortunately, though Chloe knew their relationship was deepening, she felt like an emotional schoolgirl around Braden, not a thoughtful, rational woman of 27. Was this love? And why wasn't she sure?

11 THE RING

Chloe felt thankful they had not seen Mark in the days Braden spent at Manitou Inn. But that changed the night before Braden left. Since it was their last night together, Braden took Chloe to the same restaurant they had so enjoyed during his last visit. Halfway through dinner, Chloe looked up to see Mark and Marcie being ushered past them to a table near theirs. Marcie gasped and exclaimed happily, "Why, look who's here, Mark. It's Chloe and ..." She paused artfully, giving Braden the once-over.

Chloe knew Marcie was going to milk this situation for all it was worth, and she braced herself inwardly.

"Braden, I'd like you to meet Marcie Turner and Mark Lockley. Marcie and Mark, this is Braden Willis."

Mark's face turned leaden as Braden stepped forward and shook his hand.

"We're so glad to finally meet Braden, Chloe," Marcie gushed, obviously relishing every minute. "Braden, you probably know Mark and Chloe go way back. They've been friends since childhood."

Braden's smile faded, and he glanced sideways at Chloe. Obviously, Braden was making some connections. Chloe's head was spinning. These two men meeting was a situation she was both expecting and dreading. It was bound to happen, she knew, in a small town like Pentwater. But she had pushed this thought back many times. And now that it was occurring, she felt numb emotionally, as though a decision had been made for her. Chloe moved slightly nearer to Braden and felt his arm go around her shoulders, pulling her close. She looked up at him and caught him beaming at her.

"Well, Mark," Braden said, confident again. "Chloe has mentioned you. Is your wife in town also?" he added significantly.

"I'm divorced," Mark replied shortly. "Divorced and back in Pentwater to stay. Hasn't Chloe told you that?"

Low blow, Chloe thought. But quickly looking back over the previous weeks, she knew that nothing had happened, that she had done nothing wrong—well, almost nothing, if feelings don't count. She gave Braden's hand a squeeze. He grasped hers in return, looking at her in a way that was both radiant and possessive.

"Well, we don't discuss *everything,*" Braden shot back, "especially stuff in the past."

"But the past is important," Mark countered. "Besides, my return to Pentwater is certainly in the present."

"Actually," Braden said, warming to his subject, "Chloe and I spend more time discussing the *future.*"

Touche, Chloe thought. She glanced at Marcie, whose chin had dropped, so to speak. This was not the result Marcie had intended, Braden and Mark trading barbs like this.

I could enjoy this situation, Chloe thought, *two men fighting over me*—as they obviously were—*if it were not for the fact that my future, my very life, hangs in the balance.* It perhaps was fate that had placed Mark and Braden in her life at the same point; she didn't know.

God wants me to choose, Chloe thought. The trouble was that she wasn't sure of her feelings, wasn't sure *what* she should do.

I wish I had time to sort through my emotions, Chloe thought. But she instinctively knew that, if she waffled between the two, it would only cause her heartache and she could end up forever damaging *both* relationships.

The only realistic thing to do is to stay with Braden. It just makes sense. After all, Braden was incredibly steady in his devotion to her, while Mark—*Why, I'm not even sure Mark wants me now. He has never said anything of the sort to me, like he came back to Pentwater because of me. I'm probably reading too much into the whole situation, perhaps because I want to. Once is enough for Mark to break my heart. I can't let it happen again.* There. The decision was made. Now why didn't she feel good about it?

All this time she spent thinking, Marcie had been "entertaining" Mark and Braden with some anecdote about a boy in their youth group. Both men looked bored. Soon Marcie and Mark returned to their table to order dinner. Chloe and Braden left shortly afterwards.

Once outside the restaurant, Braden chided her, "You didn't mention Mark being back in town."

"It didn't seem important," Chloe responded. This comment, of course, was what Braden wanted to hear.

"I'm glad you said that, Chloe. I hope you've put this man behind you, because I want you to focus on *us*, on our future."

After they had gotten into the car, Braden dug into his pants pocket.

"I was going to wait for the 'right time.' But with old boyfriends coming out of the woodwork, now it's going to be. Besides," he added, "I'm taking a chance on losing this carrying it around with me."

He pulled out a small box. "Anyway, here's that surprise I was telling you about."

Chloe's hands trembled as she reached for the box. She had an idea what Braden's surprise was. As she opened the box, she gasped. It was beautiful, a unique ring. One large diamond surrounded by many small diamonds in the pattern of a flower and stem was imbedded in a burnished silver band. She slipped it on her finger and was amazed that it fit.

"Braden, I don't know what to say except that I love this ring."

Braden smiled broadly.

"I special-ordered it. Of all the available patterns, this looked the most like you."

"But how did you know my size?"

I'm good at eyeballing measurements because of my work. But, frankly, there was a bit of luck involved. I'm glad it fits. Now you can put it right on and scare off hopeful suitors once and for all."

Braden took Chloe's hand, looking at her earnestly.

"You do know what I mean, don't you, Chloe? If I'm clumsy at romantic proposals of marriage, it's because I've never even been close before. But I want you in my life forever. I want you to be my wife."

Chloe dropped her eyes from his intense gaze, struggling for a response that made sense. She couldn't honestly feign surprise at his proposal because she wasn't surprised. She was just not ready to face such a decision.

"Oh, Braden, you know I care about you. But we've known each other such a short time," she exclaimed. "And there are so many issues. Where would we live? And what about Lilli and Pops?"

"Whoa, whoa," Braden said, gently pressing her hand. "Everything will work out."

"But wouldn't taking our relationship more slowly be better for both of us?" Chloe pleaded. "We've known each other—what?—two months now. And during that two months we've been together so little."

Braden's brows knit together elegantly. "Well, I know I want you to be my wife. I guess that didn't require a lot of time for *me*. I just wish you were as sure as I am."

Chloe could tell he was becoming upset. She looked

away from him and sighed.

Braden took her hands in his and continued persuasively, "I hate leaving you here, Chloe. This long-distance thing is driving me crazy."

"But I've lived here all my life, Braden. Can't you understand that?" Chloe asked, tears forming in her eyes. "I have obligations here. I *love* living in Pentwater. I don't think I could bear city life."

"That's okay. I'll create a little Pentwater for you near Chicago. Chicago is on Lake Michigan too, you know."

Chloe dabbed at her eyes, smiling, in spite of herself, at his eagerness. Still she held her ground. "But since it's *my* life we're uprooting, I'd like more time to make the adjustment."

"I'll build us a second home in Pentwater," Braden said, still in his "sales pitch" mode. "Then you can come up here in the summer. And don't forget," he added, "Lilli may be making trips to Chicago in the future to see her father. Everything might dovetail better than you think."

"Then there's Pops. He can't run Manitou Inn alone."

"Chloe, for goodness sakes, I *know* that. I know that running Manitou Inn will have to be handled in some way. I know how important Pops and Lilli are to you. For that reason alone, they're extremely important to me. But people do get married; people do move. Things will work out. They'll work out the way they're supposed to."

Chloe nodded. She fervently wished what Braden said was true, that their marriage was what was supposed to happen. But she couldn't help putting the brakes on a bit. She was tense, frustrated and not showing the dovelike submission Braden would have welcomed. Tears welled again in her eyes.

"Braden, you don't understand. Haven't you noticed Pops' attitude, how he bristles each time I'm in a relationship with a man? Somehow I can't help feeling that's because of what happened to Marie."

"I *have* noticed, and that is blatantly unfair to you," Braden said, his voice rising. "You have a right to your own life, Chloe, apart from Pops. You're 27 years old. He has to let you go."

"I know, I know," Chloe murmured. "I'm just saying let's ease into this. What if I started wearing this beautiful ring without broadcasting it as an engagement yet?"

"Okay. As long as you and I know it *is* an engagement and a certain old 'friend' named Mark realizes you're engaged."

Chloe had to smile at that. "Don't worry, Braden. I think he gets the picture."

"Oh, well. All right," Braden said with a sigh. "I guess that's something I can live with for now. But remember, Chloe, not a *long* engagement. I want our life together to begin as soon as possible."

"Yes," Chloe countered. "But I want it to start the right way. And considering Lilli and Pops and my relocating to Chicago—all big issues to me—I want to take it slowly. That's all."

Finally it was Tuesday morning, and Braden was gone. The only physical evidence of his former presence was the diamond ring sparkling on Chloe's finger. Pops dismissed it with a, "Humph. Nice," while Lilli, enthralled with its flower-and-stem shape, begged earnestly for a smaller copy of the ring. While Chloe wore the beautiful ring with pride, she wasn't yet willing to discuss its meaning with anyone. In her mind, she was trying to accept the fact she was engaged to a man she had known only a short time and that she might leave Pentwater for a new life in Chicago. It was incredible and yet, if Chloe was honest with herself, not all that unexpected. Braden had been clearly serious from the start, a fact Chloe found both frightening and irresistible. And while Chloe was deeply moved by Braden, she was having difficulty applying the logo of "love" to her emotions.

Perhaps I'm so unpracticed in the area of serious romance I find it hard to believe I'm in love, Chloe thought. Though 27 was not an advanced age, her schoolgirl dreams had long ago been replaced by the sober realities of life. *After all, I saw what happened to Marie, and then I lost Mark as well.*

Chloe couldn't help thinking about Mark and what he had meant to her. Growing up with Mark as a constant companion, Chloe had, in her mind, harbored thoughts of marrying him one day. In junior high, they had attended dances together because they did things together anyway. Through high school, they had a carefree sturdy friendship. They were young and not ready to take each other seriously. Then the prom at the end of senior year changed everything.

They went together as they had to so many dances before. Perhaps it was the beautiful dress, the corsage or the shock of seeing Mark in a tux that caused the odd sweetness when they looked at each other, as though it was for the first time. At the dance, when Mark's arms went around her, Chloe felt this was not Mark but an entrancing stranger she had loved, but not known, her entire life. And Mark's eyes reflected Chloe's surprise and enchantment. That night was different as they danced; different with their first kiss. Chloe and Mark, good friends before the Prom, were inseparable afterward. Chloe was in love. It was intense and memorable, as first love is.

Chloe knew Mark planned to attend Michigan State University that fall. She also knew by this time that she would not be leaving for college. Since taking on accounting duties for several businesses in town, plus those of Manitou Inn, and helping to run the Inn, Chloe felt no need or desire to attend a university. Mark wanted to leave Pentwater to find himself, to find his profession, while Chloe knew she had already found hers. She was happy. It would be senseless to change it. She loved her church; she loved her family; she loved walks down the beach in *any* weather. If there was a heaven on earth, Chloe was in it. The accounting and keeping Manitou Inn clean and hospitable was challenging, the scenery lovely. Pentwater was exciting and bustling in the summer and isolated with beautiful calm in the winter. Mark was wound up in her memories: fishing, stopping for candy at the store after school, swimming, sledding. They shared their childhoods, and it had been wonderful.

Now she imagined visiting Mark at Michigan State University and long vacations with him at home. As the summer heated up, so did their romance. Feeling this way about Mark bewildered Chloe. It gave him a power over her that she struggled against at times. She was jealous of him and put more weight on every nuance of his behavior. And she became emotional—angry, sad, happy—quicker than she could have imagined possible. What she liked before now she adored. He seemed to glow when he walked. Mark was her world, and it was summer. They spent afternoons on the beach and danced at the club on the edge of town. Many evenings they took long drives in Mark's father's old hunting car. In contrast to their blossoming romance was David Trassault's arrival at Manitou Inn and her sister Marie's growing fascination with him. *That turned everything turned sour for Mark and I,* Chloe thought. *We saw what trouble passion can lead to, and our love couldn't survive it.*

By summer's end the glow was gone, and Chloe's yearning had begun. Mark grew quiet, unresponsive, moody and finally stopped calling. This was particularly painful because Mark had been her best friend. That fall was a gloomy, hurting time for both Hening sisters. Mom and Pops knew what Chloe's problem was, for they were used to seeing Mark around. Marie's sadness they could not understand, until she announced her pregnancy in late fall. After that Marie's dilemma took center stage, making Chloe's broken heart, even in Chloe's estimation, less important. But silently through the years she had grieved Mark's loss, his presence in her life.

Chloe sighed. *What puzzling turns life takes,* she thought.

12 DAVID'S ANSWER

Weeks had gone by since Chloe mailed her letter to David—three and a half, to be exact. In the back of her mind churned the same questions: Would he respond? Or would silence be their only answer? Finally, the Wednesday of the week before the fall festival party, a Federal Express letter arrived, postmarked from Chicago. Chloe was alone in the house and signed for it with shaking hands. She knew it was from David.

After dashing upstairs and closing her bedroom door—totally unnecessary as Pops was busy at the hotel and Lilli in school—Chloe clumsily pulled the letter from its cardboard covering. It was a long letter, four pages in length. At first she was so nervous she couldn't make sense of it. The letters were only black lines snaking down the page. *Calm down*, she told herself and, drawing a deep breath, began to read slowly.

> *Dear Chloe:*
> *As you might imagine, I have never received a letter which shook me to the core as yours did! My first thought was of Marie and how she suffered, for Marie and my wife are the true victims here—and, of course, precious Lilli. You must believe me when I tell you I had no wish to hurt anyone. But I have*

always been one to give my passions, whatever they may be, a freer rein than I should—a sore sin indeed, which has caused everyone sadness. I want you to know I did care for Marie. I remember her vividly even now, her sweet loveliness. Now that I am older I regret the freedoms I took in my younger years, for that is what they seemed to me then, freedom. As I have matured, I have learned that you must face the consequences of your actions and, therefore, my "freedom" in recklessly treating Marie as my wife must be paid for. Marie certainly paid the price, and how sorry I am for it! I wish I had been told at the time, but I understand how Marie felt.

I'm sure you remember my son and daughter from the time we spent with you. They are now both away at college. So Chris, my wife, and I are rambling around in this big townhouse by ourselves. You'll have to excuse my delay in answering your letter. Much of it was due to the week and a half it took me to gather the courage to tell Chris. She, I'm afraid, is the "sensible one" of the family, and I rely on her love and understanding. Not surprisingly, Chris thought of a reasonable plan, which I hope you'll agree to.

Chris, after the first shock, which brought tears, is as adamant as ever you would be that Lilli's feelings be treated with care. Chris feels that she, as a new person in Lilli's life (for she wants to be part of it) and as yet a stranger, should be the one to come to Pentwater to visit Lilli and talk to you and your father about how she and I might enter Lilli's life, if you are willing. In this way, Lilli could become acquainted with Chris without the worry and/or excitement of meeting her father for the first time. This seems more natural to Chris and allows time for adult discussions before my arrival. (My wife is afraid I'll bungle things and, sad to say, she may be right.)

As for my feelings, they have evolved from extreme initial shock, to fear of telling my wife, to now joy and an impatience to see my new-found daughter. I want to make it up to Lilli for the time I missed in her life. Chris, however, insists we go slowly for Lilli's sake. I would so appreciate any pictures you have of Lilli, Chloe. My only hurdle now is how to tell my children. As you might imagine, it is a parent's nightmare to admit to his children how he has failed them and their mother. I hate spoiling or undermining their memories of that summer in Pentwater. Unfortunately, they have been through this before. So that is yet to be done. Chris will be calling you in a week or two to arrange a visit, if you are willing. I am so glad you stepped forward, Chloe, and told me about Lilli. This makes us all family, I believe!

See you soon! David Trassault

Chloe slowly put the letter down and closed her eyes. The tension drained from her body. She was almost dizzy with relief. The letter was better than Chloe dared to hope for. It brought back David Trassault before her, a happy, life-giving, magnetic man with an artist's soul, like Lilli. Chloe was comforted that his wife, Chris, wanted a place in Lilli's life too. Chloe felt sorry she had ever thought of David's wife as a cold socialite. Her one mistake had been to leave David, knowing his free-flowing personality, for such a long time. But then his children had been there too.

Life is strange, Chloe thought. But now it was time to put back some of the pieces that had gone astray. Chloe heaved a sigh of relief. Now she was convinced it *had* been right to tell David. Finally Lilli would know her father.

Chloe folded her hands and bowed her head to pray.

Thank you, God. Pops and I have worried so about

Lilli and David. In your mysterious ways, you've answered our prayers and eased our fears. I'm incredibly happy. But Pops, she thought with a start, *has to be told immediately.*

She rushed downstairs, letter in hand, and entered the hotel portion of Manitou Inn, searching for him. She found him re-grouting a tub surround in one of the rooms.

"Pops," Chloe said, waving the letter. "A letter came from David. And it sounds good; it sounds good."

Pops looked up, hitting his head on the shower bar. "What? What?" he growled, rubbing his head with his non-grouty hand. "Did you say David? It's about time. I've been going nuts. What does he say?"

Chloe shoved the letter towards him, but Pops waved it off.

"You know I can't read it without my glasses. Read it to me, will you?"

Chloe closed the door to the room and read Pops the letter, glancing at him from time to time. Pops was intent on absorbing every word. And in the end, Chloe saw in his face the same relief she was feeling.

"You're right. This is good. They seem to be willing to take it easy with us and with Lilli. My poor little girl."

"Yes," Chloe responded with a smile. "But your 'little girl' and my darling, much-loved niece is ready to meet her father, I think."

"Of course. Why shouldn't she be? Growing up without a mom or a dad, how awful."

"Well, she has a loving grandpa and a terrific aunt," Chloe reminded him. "But it can't have been easy for her. Oh, I'm so happy for Lilli."

Pops grinned broadly. "Now we'll have to 'sit on' this until his wife visits—well, actually until David himself comes, I guess. Can you keep a secret?"

"Can you?" Chloe shot back. "Of course we will keep it a secret until the proper time. You and I are good at keeping secrets, aren't we?"

Pops sighed. "Too good. Now this 'missing father' secret will come right for Lilli at last."

"I predict you and I will be the better for it."

"Yes," Pops replied. "It has weighed on me these years."

"Me too," Chloe said. "And now we can move on."

"There still could be difficulties," Pops continued with a worried look. "What if they want Lilli to live in Chicago with them full time?"

"Pops, we've got to stop worrying," Chloe said firmly. "David sent a kind, reasonable letter. This is good. Braden thinks ..."

"What's Braden got to do with this?"

Chloe sighed. "Well, naturally I've talked to Braden about this. And he ..."

"But what does he know?" Pops said insistently, his face turning red.

"I'm trying to explain. Braden feels sure—and I know he's not a lawyer—that David *can't* scoop Lilli up and take her away; that he, in fact, abandoned Lilli and Marie. And as the people Marie entrusted to care for Lilli, her grandfather and aunt, we *have* rights, since she has lived with us for so long."

"We're not the parent, though."

"That's true," Chloe agreed, attempting to soothe him. "Remember all the things we've had to put in God's hands? This is one of them. We can pray. But we'd better pray for cooperation on *all* sides, because that is what Lilli needs."

"I hate to admit it, but you're right," Pops grumbled. "I hear something good, and I have to gnaw on it. Okay. I'll be quiet now and count my blessings."

When Chloe returned to her room, she was still smiling.

On the afternoon of Lilli's fall festival party, Chloe helped Lilli dress. She took several pictures of Lilli in her ballerina's outfit. Lilli struck careful poses. Chloe hoped to develop these photos and add them, as more recent pictures, to the collection she was gathering for David. Chloe, looking at Lilli's dark beauty fondly, felt confident David would be delighted with his daughter's appearance, so much did it mirror his own. The thought was a happy one, and Chloe smiled.

"You're coming, aren't you, Chloe? You promised, remember?"

"Wouldn't miss it for the world, honey. My pretty ballerina going for a hayride and having a Halloween costume party, now that's exciting."

"We'll both have fun."

Chloe laughed with delight.

"Don't I know it."

As she and Lilli entered the church activity hall, Chloe couldn't help thinking this was the first she had seen Mark since their meeting at the restaurant last week. Marcie and Mark were welcoming the costumed children and arranging glasses of apple cider and donuts on a table. Marcie gave Chloe a smug wave and moved possessively closer to Mark, who glanced up at Chloe and then abruptly lowered his head. As the party progressed, Chloe couldn't help noticing Mark's sour mood. He was lively when he talked to the children. But when he glanced at her, his face turned somber and thoughtful. They rarely spoke.

Late afternoon turned into evening. A glimmering sun crept closer to the horizon. The wheels of the horse-drawn farm wagon creaked loudly as it bumped through potholes in the rutted road. Most of their costumes in shambles or off altogether, the children sang "Jesus Loves Me, The B-I-B-L-E" and other easy sing-a-longs. Chloe sat curled up next to Lilli in the straw, hugging her knees for warmth in the chill of evening. Lilli, whose eyelids were heavy, leaned against Chloe's shoulder. Mark sat next to Chloe in the hay, the first time he had been close to her all evening. Marcie sat on his other side, taking no chances Mark would forget her.

Suddenly Mark turned to Chloe. "So you're alone again?"

"What do you mean by that?" Chloe responded sharply, her anger rising.

"That Braden has left?"

"Yes, of course. He's left. He lives in Chicago."

"But he'll be back, I assume?"

"He'll be back," Chloe replied curtly.

"Have you seen Chloe's new ring, Mark?" Marcie broke in. "It's beautiful. I suppose this means a wedding soon, Chloe?"

Chloe merely shrugged her shoulders, determined not to give out unnecessary information.

Mark looked at her intently. "You're not going to marry that guy, are you, Chloe?"

"Why not?" Chloe responded tartly. "I can marry or not marry whom I please."

"But didn't you say yourself you haven't known him that long?"

"You're talking about marriage, not me," Chloe reminded him.

"Then you're not going to marry him?"

"I'll do exactly what I please," Chloe responded, exasperated.

"That's not the question."

"Let it go, Mark," Chloe snapped.

"Yes, Mark," Marcie said. "Let's talk about something—anything—more pleasant. Not that your marrying Braden wouldn't be pleasant, Chloe," she added with a smile.

No doubt, Chloe thought. *Then you would have Mark all to yourself.* Chloe settled back into the straw, noticing that Mark continued to stare at her. He looked ready to explode.

Chloe, to forestall further bickering on his part, remarked caustically, "I don't see how what I do concerns you in the least, Mark."

Mark took the hit with a slight grimace.

"Perhaps not," he said. "But I know you. And you won't be happy with that guy in Chicago."

"Really?" Chloe said angrily. "You forget, Mark, when you knew me I was in high school; a child, really. In the years since you saw me last, I've grown up. So don't presume you know me that well."

Lilli huddled closer to Chloe and began to gently squeeze Chloe's fingers with her hand, as if to divert Chloe's attention from Mark. The other children's noise turned to murmuring. Chloe sensed they had started to focus on their conversation. Mark, realizing they were creating a scene, turned to the children. He smiled and relaxed once more, totally ignoring Chloe.

But when she and Lilli about to get into the car, Mark walked over and stubbornly leaned against the door. Lilli, sensing conflict, took off to join the other children, who were waiting for their parents to pick them up.

Mark reached out and laid his hand on Chloe's arm.

"Chloe, I'm sorry. I know I have no business interfering in your life at this point."

"True," Chloe said emphatically. "You don't."

"It's just that I know now that sometimes you can't leave your past behind you."

"Though you, for example, certainly tried."

"I tried. And it was the biggest mistake of my life."

"Well," Chloe replied sharply, "that doesn't mean it will be the biggest mistake of *my* life. We aren't the same person, you know."

"Chloe," Mark said, giving her arm a gentle shake with the hand that still held it. "I know you're still angry with me. But you're making a terrible mistake."

Chloe pulled her arm away. "No. As you've said, *you're* the one who made the mistake," she said, her voice rising in decibels.

Glancing around, she saw they were again attracting

attention. She continued in a lower voice. "And this is hardly the time or place to discuss it."

"You're absolutely right," Mark agreed. "When can I see you? We need to talk."

Chloe hesitated. If she was honest with herself, she had to admit Mark was only voicing some of the doubts she herself harbored about Braden and leaving Pentwater for Chicago. She was afraid of touching base with Mark on such personal matters, as her feelings for him were far from dead. Chloe was confused enough without having a tete-a-tete with Mark. It was blatantly unfair to Braden. As if to remind herself of her engagement, Chloe gently rubbed the ring with her thumb.

"I'm sorry, Mark, but I'm too busy right now for personal discussions. And Braden is coming this weekend. I've lived my life without your input for so long I don't see how your opinion is going to help me now."

Mark sighed. "I'll catch you later, then," he said and walked back to the group of children.

13 ENGAGED!

Chloe could tell that Braden was not going to allow her too much time to get used to being engaged. Every night when he called he kept asking if she had told Pops and Lilli yet.

"I've showed them the ring, Braden. Don't you think that's pretty self-explanatory?"

"Not at all. Maybe they think I just like to give you expensive jewelry; which, of course, I do."

Chloe had to smile at his nonsense.

"Yes. But you have a purpose behind your generosity."

"Of course I do. I want to marry you as soon as possible. Then you'll get everything I have. Why? Do you want more physical evidence of my affection?"

"What on earth are you talking about?" Chloe said with a laugh.

"I don't know. Maybe you need more presents to hurry you along."

"No, I don't."

"A new sports car, French perfume, dozens of roses each and every day?"

"Don't you dare," Chloe said. "You know I'm not that type."

"Probably one of your better qualities," Braden

admitted, "but whatever it takes."

"You promised me we'd go slow," Chloe pleaded. "It's been just a few days since we've become engaged. I'm not even used to the word 'engaged' yet. Braden, this is not slow."

"Okay. I lied."

"Braden, come on. I'm serious."

"And *I'm* serious too, serious about our wedding."

"Wedding? We haven't even talked about a wedding. Braden, you're impossible," Chloe said with a sigh.

"I merely want you to tell your father and Lilli that we're engaged," Braden coaxed. "That's only reasonable, isn't it? You said they needed to be prepared. Well, give them the information so they can start getting prepared."

"But not for a wedding in two weeks or even two months," Chloe said firmly.

"Okay," Braden agreed. "But not a day over six months. Then I'd say your cold feet were turning icy."

"All right," Chloe said.

"And I'm going to tell my parents immediately."

"Braden! They're going to be so shocked."

"Sure they will. They're used to thinking of me as a perennial bachelor. They'll be delighted—grandchildren."

"Braden! Look at your progression."

"Okay. Okay. Forget I said that—for now. But I am going to tell them. Okay?"

"I guess so," Chloe said with a sigh. She could not imagine Braden's parents being "delighted" with this news at all. From her slight experience with them, they seemed like society people who would only welcome an "advantageous" alliance with a prominent family. Chloe felt they would be disappointed, if anything, with Braden's choice. And these would be her in-laws—not a very comforting thought.

"Promise me you'll tell your father and Lilli tonight."

"I promise, only to keep you from bugging me about

it," Chloe said, clearly exasperated. "I'm sure they understand ..."

"Tell them."

"Okay. Okay. I promise. Tonight I'll tell them."

"Good girl. And give me their reaction tomorrow. You remember I'm coming this weekend. Then we can talk to them together. But I want you to tell them first in private so they can voice any concerns they have."

"I understand. That's a good idea."

"Goodbye, love. Talk to you tomorrow."

Chloe hung up the phone. She looked at the pictures of Lilli scattered on her bed that she was collecting for David: Lilli as a chubby baby in Grandma's arms; Lilli splashing in the waves at 3; Lilli dressed for her first dance recital. Where had the years gone? And lately, anticipating this big change in her life, time slipped by quicker than ever. There was no turning back, no matter how much she tried to dig her toes in the sand. And her feeble stall at telling the people she loved most was only that and, of course, accomplished nothing. She would tell Pops and Lilli tonight.

But that evening, after she had blurted out her news, Pops and Lilli were more agreeable than Chloe anticipated.

"I'm so excited," Lilli squealed, jumping up and down. "You and Braden are getting married. Can I be your flower girl?"

"Of course, dear."

"When is the wedding going to be, Chloe?" Pops asked. "This spring, summer?"

Chloe glanced at Pops' face cautiously. His expression was genuinely benevolent, perhaps because he was happy Braden was making a true commitment to her, unlike David and Marie's situation. *Also*, Chloe thought, *it moved the care and upkeep of Manitou Inn right into the family*. In any case, this response boded well for Pops' future attitude toward Braden. Chloe was glad to see an end to his negativity.

"I don't know, Pops—within six months. Braden is eager for the wedding to take place as soon as possible."

"That's good. I've never thought much of long engagements. Your mother and I, of course, had to wait a few years because we were so young when we met."

"That's what I mean," Chloe said, thoroughly floored by Pops' apparent change of heart. "You and Mom knew each other a long time before you married. That's why I tell Braden we should wait a bit and get to know each other better."

"Humph," Pops grunted derisively. "How long do you need? I knew I wanted to marry your mother two weeks after I met her, and I was 15 years old. You and Braden are older, no schooling to take care of, no real obstacles. Why wait?"

Pops peered at Chloe more closely.

"Unless you're not sure you want to marry him, Chloe. Only you can answer that. Now, that's a different story."

"Oh, Grandpa, Chloe *loves* Braden," Lilli chimed in, all her former coolness about Braden forgotten. "The kids think he is soooo cute. And I get to be in their wedding. Are you going to have a big wedding, Chloe?"

Then Lilli's face fell. She had thought of something.

"You won't go away, will you, Chloe?"

"I'm afraid so, dear. I'll have to live in Chicago with Braden."

"Oh, no. Don't go," Lilli cried, her eyes filling with tears. "Or"—she looked uncertainly between Pops and Chloe—"take me with you."

She started to wail.

"You can't leave, Chloe. What will I do for a mom?"

Chloe started to cry too and threw her arms around the sobbing girl.

"I don't want to leave you. I can't leave you."

Pops looked on doubtfully. "Now, *there's* your obstacle, Chloe."

"I know, I know," Chloe sniffled, holding onto Lilli tightly. "I just can't leave Lilli and you—and Pentwater. I was meant to live here, I think. Oh, Pops, what am I going to do?"

Pops looked thoughtful.

"Well, we've always been a crazy patchwork family. But if you love this man, we'll work something out."

Where had Chloe heard this before, "We'll work something out"? Hadn't Braden said the same thing?

"Chicago isn't that far away. You could come back for long weekends, holidays. Lilli could spend time in Chicago—or you up here—during the summers." Pops was thinking. "You certainly won't have to work. Braden seems quite able to support you. Surely you could come to Pentwater a lot. We won't rent out your room."

"But I love my job. How will you manage Manitou Inn without me?"

Chloe couldn't believe this. While she wallowed in negativity, Pops was being positive about her marrying Braden.

"Hire more people, I guess. Business has been good lately. And now that it isn't a family business any more—but it is, isn't it? After all, Braden will be family too."

Chloe's suspicions had been correct. Pops hadn't forgotten that aspect, of Manitou Inn being managed intra-family, so to speak. At his age, however, he could hardly be blamed. It must feel like a tremendous burden being lifted from his shoulders, and this done without him leaving Manitou Inn in the care of strangers.

"I'd like to go to Chicago, Chloe," Lilli said. "Will you take me to see some famous artists' paintings?"

"Sure, honey, sure."

Chloe thought that Pops and Lilli were having less difficulty making accommodations than she was. *But then,* she thought bitterly, *I'm the one who's leaving.*

"If you love Braden, Chloe, it's going to work out. Lilli and I will be around. You won't lose Manitou Inn or Pentwater. Besides," Pops said with a smile, "maybe it's time for an addition to this family—and perhaps more to follow."

He's into grandchildren too, Chloe thought. *I can't believe it.*

"Well. Okay," she said. What else could she say? "Braden's coming this weekend. We'll talk more then."

"And don't worry," Pops said. "Everything will turn out fine."

That night, when Braden called, Chloe was happy to give him the good news, for it was good news. Chloe didn't know how she could cope with Braden's pushing on one end and her family's resistance on the other. Thank goodness that was not going to be the case. It was apparent the only uncertainty Chloe would have to deal with was her own.

The next weekend, when Braden arrived, everything was different. For one thing, Lilli rushed out to meet him when he arrived, darting around Chloe, who was standing at the door. As Braden clambered out of his car, Lilli leaped up on him, throwing her arms around his neck.

"You're getting married; you're getting married. Can I call you Uncle Braden now? Or—you're really sort of my dad, aren't you?"

Braden grinned broadly. "Yes, Lilli. In a way you could say that."

"Oh, won't the kids be jealous! I have a dad-uncle who lives in Chicago."

Braden burst out laughing, untangling Lilli's arms from about his neck, but holding her hand as they walked towards Chloe.

"A dad-uncle, huh?" he said. "Say, I like the sound of that."

"Me too," Chloe said, stroking the top of Lilli's dark

hair. "There aren't many of those around these days."

"Oh, no," Lilli said seriously. "That's special."

"Well," Chloe said, bending down to kiss Lilli's cheek, "I think *you're* the one who's special."

"I know," Lilli said, and disappeared into the house.

Chloe was just able to drag Braden into the house before he gave her one of their long "hello" kisses. When they finally drew apart, who appeared in the living room but Pops, a broad smile creasing the corners of his mouth. Chloe thought he looked years younger. She would have never guessed it. Had Pops a secret desire to get rid of her through marriage all these years?"

"I hear congratulations are in order," he said, holding his hand out to Braden. "Welcome to the Hening family. I saw Lilli bounding around."

Braden grasped his hand firmly. "I'm a lucky guy."

"We're lucky too," Pops responded genially. "It will be nice having another man around after only women all these years. When you have daughters, you get your sons through marriage."

As the weekend progressed, Chloe saw Pops' and Braden's relationship grow stronger after Pops' fears for her had disappeared. Chloe realized how lonely it must have been for Pops to run a business by himself. She helped Pops with the accounting aspects and pickup chores around Manitou Inn. But Braden, a businessman like Pops, knew what it took to run a hotel, make necessary repairs, buy products and cut costs. Chloe loved how Braden beamed when Pops teasingly called him "son."

Lilli, still delighted, nestled next to Braden while they were watching television and asked him countless questions about Chicago and "what he did," storing up information like a squirrel gathering nuts in order to impress her friends at school. Braden promised to take her to all the museums and art shows. He also guaranteed Lilli that, when she stayed with them in

Chicago after the wedding, she would have her own room. This threw Lilli into the joyful planning and decorating of this "new" room, down to painting a mural on the walls. Braden also told her that her cat, Edgar, was welcome whenever she came to Chicago.

When they were alone that night, sitting on the sofa, Braden began to act like a sultan, flushed as he was with his success of the day. After about an hour of intense kissing and embracing, during which Braden passionately pushed for closer and more, a flushed Chloe, clumsily adjusting her clothes, begged for a timeout.

"Braden, I can't take much more of this."

"Neither can I, Chloe. This isn't natural. We have to be one."

"We should be building our relationship—the emotional relationship, knowing each other better. Then the physical relationship will follow."

"Chloe, I want to be close to you in *every* way—physically, emotionally—everything."

"Then why don't you listen to me?" Chloe said, close to tears. "I told you I don't want to be with you like a wife until we're married."

"But now we're engaged. What does it matter?" Braden reached out and stroked Chloe's hair. "You know, honey, the strange thing is, when we're together like this, I swear you want it as much as I do. And you're certainly not a tease. You know I love you, and we're engaged. So what's the problem?"

"But we're not married."

"But we're going to be married."

"Oh, Braden," Chloe said with a sigh, "I wish you knew the Lord, that you believed as I do. Then you'd know why it's so wrong."

"Isn't that a little outdated?" Braden suggested gently.

This shook all the fogginess out of her head.

"The Bible is the most up-to-date, relevant book for human life there is."

Braden held up his hands.

"Okay. Okay. No lecture, please. I'll back off. I don't understand. But I'll respect my lady's wishes, hard as it is for me."

"If you attended church more often, you'd come to understand. You have to have an open heart, Braden."

"Well, my heart is open to *you.* So maybe some of this will seep into me just by being near you."

Braden was voicing a secret hope she cherished, that Braden would come to know the Lord and his ways through her. Unfortunately, Chloe knew she was not always the best example of what to do or say, try as she might. She struggled every day with her own inadequacies.

But I love the Lord, she thought. *How I pray Braden will come to know him too.* Her love of God was such a large part of Chloe's life that it was inconceivable to her that her husband would not believe. She wanted to hold out great hope for Braden, but such comments as these distressed her. How much easier and better it would be if they both felt the same way in this vital area of her life—and of his too, though he didn't seem to realize it.

Later, as they sat together actually *watching* TV, Braden behaving himself admirably and Chloe a little more at peace, she wondered if it was part of God's plan that she bring Braden to him. In this confusing romantic flurry, with doubts swirling in her mind, the thought comforted her.

14 TALKING IT OUT

The next day, with Braden gone and Chloe in the office again tackling her accounts, the phone rang. Chloe picked it up with the standard greeting.

"Hello, Manitou Inn at Pentwater. May I help you?"

A well-modulated voice asked, "May I speak to Chloe Henning, please?"

"This is she."

"My name is Chris Trassault, Ms. Hening. I'm sure you remember my husband David's letter to you, just as I remember your letter to him."

David's wife. Chloe looked at her hands. They actually started to tremble as she gripped the phone tighter. She tried to force her voice into bright friendliness, though this telephone call—and what was to come—frightened her.

"Oh, Mrs. Trassault, Chris, I'm so glad to talk to you."

"And I'm glad to finally put a voice with the letter. I'm sure that was a difficult letter for you to write. And you can understand what a difficult letter it was for me to read."

"Of course. I'm so sorry," Chloe blurted out, not knowing what else to say.

"You did the right thing, of course," Chris Trassault said shortly. "And how is our precious Lilli?"

"Fine," Chloe breathed, relaxing somewhat. "I sent you and David some pictures of her yesterday. I'm sorry they're a little late, but I got involved in digging around and ..."

"We can't wait to see her, both in pictures and in person," David's wife interrupted softly. "I—we—would have called sooner, but we've been involved in telling our children and coping with their reaction. They're old enough to understand everything fully. That's been part of the problem."

"I can imagine," Chloe said with compassion.

"It has been difficult. Our son and daughter adore their father and are very close to him. When something like this arises—and this is not the first time—it hurts them deeply, especially since they remember your sister and that summer they spent in Pentwater."

Chloe couldn't help asking, "You said, 'This is not the first time.' Do you mean ..."

"Yes. David has strayed before and ..."

"... fathered another child?" Chloe finished incredulously.

"Yes," Chris said with a hint of sadness in her voice, "a boy. He is 13 years old now, and lives with his mother. We haven't seen him in years, though David contributes to his support. His mother is hostile and wants to keep him away from David. So you see," Chris Trassault continued, "unfortunately this is not a new situation for us. But it hurts our son and daughter and, of course, myself when it happens."

"I can imagine," breathed Chloe. "And I'm so sorry to be the bearer of such upsetting news."

"Hopefully," Chris continued crisply, "we're beyond the upsetting part. Even our son and daughter are gradually becoming more mellow and wondering about their little half-sister. For my part, I'm eager to see her and welcome her into our family." She hesitated. "Perhaps you wonder how I can tolerate my husband's behavior and still stay in the marriage?"

106

"Why, n-no," Chloe stammered, unsure of how to respond.

"It's a fair question, and one I've wondered about for years. I guess the truth is I can't imagine life without David. And then he is always so sorry. He has so much to give, such a charmer. Perhaps that's part of his problem."

Chloe silently nodded her head in agreement.

"Being his wife is humiliating—but also wonderful, if you can believe that. It's never dull." There was a pause during which Chloe found she could add nothing and Chris Trassault seemed to be regrouping.

"But now on to brighter things ... like our Lilli. Your letter was full of love for Lilli. Can you bring yourself to share her a little with us?"

"Oh, yes," Chloe said happily. "Lilli needs to know her father ... and you too," she added clumsily.

"She needs all of us," Chris said firmly. "A child needs all the love he or she can get."

"Definitely," Chloe agreed, warming to this conversation.

"I imagine she is a bright, sparkling little thing, being David's daughter."

"She is," Chloe said. "She resembles David both in looks and talent. She inherited his artistic ability. She is definitely her father's child."

"Then their meeting will be dynamic and should be arranged as soon as possible. First, however, you get me. I know David told you of my plan. I scanned his letter."

"Yes," Chloe said.

"I would like to come as soon as it is convenient for you."

"Almost any time is fine. You come first in our plans."

Chloe could sense Chris' smile on the other end of the line.

"Then you're as eager as I am. Am I too pushy—I

know this is Monday—to suggest a visit next Monday, only a week away?"

"Oh, that's fine," Chloe said breathlessly. "Mondays are slow at the hotel, especially in November, when it's our off season. That will allow Pops and I more free time. And you can talk to Lilli when she returns from school."

"I have checked air schedules for Monday. There is a plane that arrives at 9:00 a.m. from Chicago into the Ludington airport. After getting a rental car, I imagine I could get to Manitou Inn about 10:00 a.m., if that is all right with you."

"Oh, let us pick you up."

"Oh, no, my dear. A rental car is fine. Heaven knows I'm used to them. I am hoping for some private time with you and your father before I talk to Lilli."

"We will make sure that happens," Chloe said seriously. "Nothing is more important to Pops and I than talking with you."

"I imagine. So I will see you around 10:00 a.m. Monday, unless something untoward happens, which I doubt."

"See you then. Goodbye," Chloe said.

She slowly laid the phone down. Chilled prickles went up and down her spine. Chris Trassault sounded decisive but kind on the phone. But would she be special enough to care for Lilli without Chloe or Pops around? *Slow down,* Chloe told herself. *You're not at that point yet.*

She went to tell Pops, who checked his calendar to make sure it was free. "Just a normal day. I'll put Charlie on notice to fill in for me that day."

"He's totally capable. I don't know why you don't do it more," Chloe said.

"I'll need time to examine this woman who *might* care for Lilli in the future. I'm usually a good judge of character. Luckily, Lilli is old enough to tell us anything that bothers her. It would take me about a half an hour to book a flight to Chicago and scoop her up, if necessary."

"And I would be right with you," Chloe agreed. "She sounds nice, very intelligent and capable. But I can't wait until Monday when we'll see for ourselves."

"What do we tell Lilli?"

"I'm sure we'll discuss that with Chris Trassault. That's most likely the reason she wants to talk to us before she sees Lilli. Pops, have your questions ready for her, as I will. This meeting is as important as David at our door. Chris Tressault will do the mothering when Lilli is with them. If Lilli goes to Chicago, David will be working for much of the day."

"That's a difficult task for a woman, to care for her husband's love child," Pops mused.

"The whole situation must be humiliating and terribly hurtful for her. She admitted as much to me over the phone. But she is obviously standing by David, and seems positive about Lilli."

"And who couldn't be positive about Lilli? She's a angel and innocent, innocent of everything," Pops blustered.

"True, true. But a lot of women wouldn't react the way Mrs. Trassault has. In fact, it's kind of amazing she is still Mrs. Trassault. She seems ready to welcome Lilli into their family. That, of course, is what we wanted all along."

"So that jerk, David, gets away with it again."

Chloe paused significantly. "Chris told me David fathered another child out of wedlock before Lilli, a boy. He's 13 years old now and lives with his mother."

"I'm not surprised. Perhaps there are others Chris doesn't know of."

"Let's hope not, Pops. And there's no sense in being bitter. David is the only father Lilli has, the only parent she has."

"Unfortunately. How I wish Marie had lived and married some decent guy. Then we could keep Lilli out of all this mess."

Chloe looked thoughtful.

"I don't know Chris Trassault at all. But from this phone call, she appears used to making David's messes right. She *does* sound thoughtful and sensible to me. And David is not all bad. I remember him as being kind and happy."

"He ruined my daughter's life. Marie might be alive today if not for that man," Pops said, wiping a tear from his eye.

It burned Chloe's heart to bring that subject up with Pops. But, after all, this revolved around Marie and David's relationship. She put her arm around Pops' shoulders.

"I hate to say this, Pops, but Marie made that choice as well as David."

"I need to be reminded of that, Chloe. But she was so young," he added wistfully.

"Well, it does no good to rehash the past. What's done is done. Now we have to do the best we can for Lilli."

"And the best includes getting her father back for her, if we can," Pops agreed.

"She'll be so excited," Chloe said.

When Lilli burst through the doorway from school that day, Chloe was there to scoop her up in her arms. Lilli wriggled free, exclaiming, "Stop. You're squeezing me, Chloe. I'm hungry. Look what I made in art, a squirrel holding a real nut."

Chloe reluctantly relinquished her hold and, looking at the picture, wondered in how many students' pictures today the squirrel looked almost more realistic than the nut.

How extraordinary Lilli is, she thought, her heart brimming with pride. No matter what difficulties lay in store, Chloe suddenly felt a warm glow that the circle of love around this remarkable child she loved was going to grow, and grow by the addition of a whole family. That is what she fervently prayed, that their family had increased. It was as though she was coming out of a dark tunnel into the light of day. The dark tunnel, which contained Marie's and Mom's deaths and the keeping of the secret, was becoming brighter, now that the truth was known. At last they were moving into the future, a future filled with hope and love.

The next day, a Tuesday, Chloe was busy in both mind and body with Chris Trassault's arrival. Suddenly the family area of Manitou Inn looked dirty and shabby to her. So she set about cleaning it, even buying new throw rugs for the kitchen area. Lilli's room got a thorough cleaning. That was a room that needed picking up every day. Lilli, upon entering her room after school on Tuesday, was surprised and generally pleased with its sparkling new appearance, though she had certain complaints.

"How am I ever going to find my easel colors now, Chloe?"

"It should be easy, honey. Now they're in the tray, where they belong."

"But I was used to them where I put them," Lilli said. "I'll never be able to find them now."

"Well, I want you to keep them picked up, Lilli, and not strew them all over the floor again."

"Why not?"

"Why? Because your room needs to stay clean for awhile. That's why."

"But nobody cares. Melanie doesn't care. I don't care."

Chloe sucked in her breath. *Here goes*, she thought.

"Someone special is visiting us next Monday, a lady."

"You mean some lady we don't know is going to come snooping around in my room?"

"Not necessarily, honey. I just want the house clean, including your room."

"Well, I'll try," Lilli said, already searching in the easel tray for the displaced colors.

About noon on Wednesday, as Chloe was in the midst of dusting off book covers in the office area, the phone rang. Chloe, feather duster in hand, ran to answer it.

"Chloe, this is Mark."

Chloe didn't need to be told. The sound of Mark's voice, even after the years they spent apart, was so familiar to Chloe she would recognize it anywhere.

"Yes, Mark?" she said coolly, remembering their irate discussion at the fall festival party.

"I want you to forgive me for my behavior at the party. I had no business snapping at you like that."

Chloe sighed. "You're right. You didn't."

Mark continued. "I just got upset because—listen, Chloe, I've got to talk to you."

"Why, Mark? What could you possibly have to say to me *now*?"

"I know you think I have no business in your life, and maybe you're right. But we've been friends for a long time. And I need to have closure on this."

"Closure on what?" Chloe said, becoming angry. "I thought you had closure when you stopped calling me, when you left Pentwater for college and I never heard from you. I would *think* you had closure when you married. I don't understand what you're talking about, Mark."

"Chloe, can I see you tonight? I don't want our relationship to end this way, in bitterness."

"Mark, our relationship ended after high school, during the summer after high school."

"But I'm here now."

"And what difference does that make? Do you think I've been just sitting here waiting for you to return? Do you think I've said to myself, 'Well, Mark never calls or writes, but soon he will return to Pentwater and we will take up where we left off'? Do you think I said that to myself when I found out you had married?"

"I've made some mistakes, Chloe. I just don't want you to make the same ones."

"Well, thank you very much, but I will handle my life as I see fit. I've been doing it, without any help from you, for years."

"Please, Chloe, I'm begging you. Let me take you out for dinner tonight so we can really talk. Then you can humiliate me properly for leaving you after high school."

"Mark, I don't want to humiliate you. It's just that—well, my life is in an upheaval now, with my engagement ..."

"So you *are* engaged."

"Yes," Chloe replied shortly "... and reconnecting Lilli with her father and ..."

"Chloe, I'm begging you, as an old friend, if we've ever had any good times together—and you know we have—not to exclude me from your life right now. Maybe I can help you. I still know you, Chloe. I understand where you're coming from more than most people, even after the time we've been apart."

This comment sent chills down Chloe's spine, for it was true. She would never admit it to Mark, but she felt a connection to him, a tie, even when he was gone. Because of it, she had suffered greatly in his absence. It frightened her to feel he knew this, especially now that she was determined to take a new path away from the past and its hurtful memories. If he knew her, then he knew that she still loved him, would always love him. In that moment, Chloe faced the truth. It hit her like a brick. She loved Mark. But he had betrayed her, betrayed her totally. It made her sure that he didn't return her love and wasn't worthy of her love.

Chloe's serene, if a bit sad, life of a few months ago had become chaotic and quick-changing. She knew talking to Mark had dangers. But she found herself saying with a sigh, "All right."

"I'll be at Manitou Inn at 6:00 p.m. See you then,"

Mark said, hanging up before Chloe could change her mind.

That evening she fed Pops and Lilli quickly.

"Why aren't you eating, Chloe?" Pops asked.

"Oh, Mark Langley is taking me out for supper. He wants to talk," Chloe said, looking at Pops' face for his reaction. But Pops was serene.

"Fine," he said. "Don't be too late."

"Can you tell Braden, when he calls, I'm out with a friend and I'll call him tomorrow night?"

"Yup," Pops said calmly.

"And could you not mention it's Mark?" Chloe continued with some embarrassment. "Braden doesn't like him."

"No problem."

Chloe wondered what Pops really thought about this. But she was glad he was staying aloof from her problems. Her own conscience would have to bear the brunt of seeing Mark tonight. *Nothing is wrong; nothing is wrong,* she kept telling herself. But she knew something was wrong, and what was wrong came from deep inside of her.

At 6:00 p.m. Chloe was at the front door, waiting, when Mark walked up the front path. His dark, curly hair, broad shoulders and easy walk were all so familiar. She even half turned her face away to avoid the sweet ache she felt when looking at him. She would have to be very firm, very sure. He must be put in his place, the place he belonged, in her past, far away from her future life with Braden. *Oh, God,* she prayed, *give me strength.* And then, *Why does this have to be so difficult? And what does he want to talk about anyway?*

Why did he have to take a hold of her arm? And why did it feel so natural, so right? Why did she have the feeling he exuded a magnetic field whose force drew her to him? She knew beforehand this evening wasn't going to help her confusion about Braden.   But she was determined not to give up a man who loved her for somebody who had dumped her unceremoniously years before.

"Where are we going?" Chloe asked after Mark began driving southward.

"The Sea Shell Bar and Grill.   They have great steaks."

"Did you discover this place with Marcie?"

"Don't go there, Chloe," Mark replied brusquely.   "You know she means nothing to me."

His reply silenced Chloe.   She looked at the Lake Michigan shoreline as they drove.   A delicate, faintly yellow November sun was being eclipsed by steely gray clouds as it made its way to the horizon.   *How bleak everything looks,* she thought grimly.   *I wish I had taken a stroll on the beach, anything other than being with Mark tonight.   What am I doing here?*   She glanced at Mark's silhouette as he drove.   He looked somber, a warning this evening would not be light and casual.

Well, he'll have his say and I'll have mine, Chloe thought, resisting an impulse to run.   *I was a fool to come tonight.*

The Sea Shell Bar and Grill was rustic and filled with sea memorabilia.   There were peanut shucks on the floor and a large group of noisy, partying locals.

"I picked this place because, when you start yelling at me, it won't be heard above the din.   I want you to yell at me, Chloe, to get it all out."

"What good would that do?"

"Clear the air between us, so we can get around it."

"Get around what?"

"You know you're still upset with me, Chloe.   It's obvious."

"What should be obvious is I'm engaged to another man and I am not the same girl you knew before."

Mark held up his hand.   "Okay.   Okay.   Settle down.

I know you're engaged. I just wanted to see you tonight to tell you how I feel. I want you to know I love you."

Chloe began to sputter.

"All right. All right. I know I shouldn't be saying this. But it's true. It kills me that you think otherwise. I've made some terrible decisions, and I know I deserve to pay for them. I've run from my feelings for you. I don't know why. Maybe our feelings for each other got too deep too soon for me. Maybe I'd always yearned to leave Pentwater, to see what the rest of the world was like. We're so isolated here."

"I love Pentwater, the life here," Chloe said, stunned and close to tears.

"I love it too. But I had to leave it to learn I loved it, where you always knew. And I'll have to say that what went on between Marie and David scared me. I guess that just added to the fact that I needed to get away; to grow up, so to speak."

"Are you trying to tell me you stopped seeing me, never called or wrote, married someone else, yet you loved me all the time? That doesn't make sense at all. That's ridiculous."

"At first I thought I needed distance from Pentwater and from you. I wanted new experiences. And I loved college. That might offend you, but there it is. I was having the time of my life. I dated Susan, who was so different from you. She seemed a part of my big, new life; no more small town boy, you see. I still thought about you. But I avoided seeing you again because I wanted to change. I was afraid of the effect seeing or speaking to you again would have on me. My parents told me about Lilli's birth and Marie and your Mom dying, and that, selfishly, scared me. Life was fun and exciting, and I wanted to keep it that way."

"Those were awful times for me," Chloe said, fighting back tears.

"I knew that. But, again, for me being away seemed good. I was too young to want the responsibility of entering that sad situation. Later, after I had married and the marriage began to sour, I thought of Pentwater and you more and more and yearned to come back to the values and the life I led before. My new life, even my job, seemed artificial and rather crass to me. I knew I had taken the wrong direction. And that wrong direction began when I foolishly left the most important person in my life, you."

Mark took Chloe's hands in his, looking at her tenderly.

"I'm begging you to forgive me, Chloe. I know I don't deserve a second chance. But I'm hoping, if you search your heart, you'll realize we were meant to be together."

They spent a few moments gazing at each other. Every fiber in Chloe's being wanted to forgive him, to be with him. But she shook her head as if to clear it, and pulled her hands away.

"It's too late, Mark. Sometimes things happen in life that can't be erased, can't be 'made right.' I'm afraid this is one of them. I understand how you felt, wanting a new life of your own. I know that I'll always care a great deal about you. I wish things had worked out differently between us. But I've suffered too. And I think it's time I began a new life with a new person and leave my often-sad past behind."

"I was afraid you'd say that, Chloe. But this Braden guy is such a smooth city type, dressed for success and all. I can't see you with him."

"Little country bumpkin me?"

"He couldn't do better than you, no matter *where* he looked," Mark said staunchly.

"Funny thing is, I think he feels the same way," Chloe said. As she said this, she knew how she appreciated and needed Braden's unquestioned love. She wore it like a badge of honor. His love lifted her up, made her feel special.

"But how will you survive leaving Pentwater?"

This hit Chloe in a tender spot, a frontrunner of her

worries about the marriage. She answered quickly, "Like I've survived everything else. Braden promised me a house here. I'll be in Pentwater often, with my family."

"I don't see him much in church. Is this a guy that loves the Lord?"

"He's just beginning the path, Mark. We were all beginners at one time."

"But I wonder if he is just putting on a good front about religion to get you to marry him. You know how difficult marriage is, Chloe, without God at the center of it. I only have to look at my own marriage. I hate to see you dealing with a husband who doesn't believe."

Mark probed her misgivings like open wounds. But Chloe was resistant to this tactic coming from him, a divorced man who she was sure, as most human beings, had compromised his values from time to time. Besides, she knew what he was trying to do, tear down Braden in every way he could. And she would have none of it.

"I'm sure you can't see into Braden's heart to know *what* his relationship with God is. And it's an issue for me to deal with, without any counseling from you."

"You can see through me, I guess. I'm desperate to have you see it's me and not Braden who can make you happy. But I see it isn't working. I guess you're as stubborn about making a mistake as I was. Then I'll see you in church now and again," Mark remarked quietly. "That will be my punishment, living in Pentwater and seeing you occasionally, married with children."

"I hope we can be friends, Mark," Chloe said uncertainly.

"Much more than friends," Mark replied sadly. "I want you to remember, if you ever need me, I'm there for you."

"I'll remember."

They were silent on their way home, each lost in his own thoughts. At the door of Manitou Inn, Mark took Chloe in his arms and gave her a soft kiss on the cheek.

"Just remember this, Chloe, I love you and always will."

Chloe longed to say, "I love you" back to Mark. But she felt it was improper. Her heart ached for him—and herself—as he turned and walked slowly towards his car.

"The end again," she thought, "for a second time," and sadly let herself into the house.

15 LILLI'S NEW FAMILY

On Monday Pops and Chloe started their morning tasks as usual. But by 9:30 they gave up all pretence of normalcy and hovered near the front door, anxiously awaiting Chris Trassault's arrival. At 10:11 the doorbell rang. Chloe answered it to find a thin, tallish woman with graying brown hair cut extremely short and large deep brown eyes that regarded her with a kind expression. Chris Trassault immediately held out her hand.

"You must be Chloe. I'm Chris Trassault, David's wife."

"I'm happy to meet you," Chloe said sincerely. "Please come in. Let me introduce you to my father."

Pops stepped forward and shook Mrs. Trassault's hand. Chris Trassault was dressed neatly in a tan pantsuit. Her dark eyes studied Pops and Chloe minutely, as they did her, while a gentle smile played on her lips.

"It's good to meet you at last," she said. "And I want to thank you for the adorable pictures of Lilli. She is a little beauty. You must be so proud."

"And good as gold," Pops said staunchly.

"We love her so," Chloe added unnecessarily.

"I'm sure you do. And I know you want to assure

yourself that David and I will love and care for Lilli if you allow her to visit us occasionally."

Pops and Chloe looked at each other.

"Yes" they said together.

"That's why we need to know and trust each other, which brings me here today. Have you told Lilli anything about my coming to Pentwater?"

"I told her a lady was coming today to visit. And I made her promise to keep her room neat," Chloe said with a sheepish laugh.

"That's a start," Chris replied. "How would it be if, at our first meeting, Lilli is just given my first name? That way I can get to know her a little before she finds out I am her father's wife."

"Fine," Chloe said.

"But Lilli is bound to ask questions," Pops added. "And we will have to give her truthful answers."

"Certainly," Chris said. "In fact, within ten minutes of meeting Lilli, I have a feeling she will, in her own way, learn who I am—the truth, absolutely. I just want a tiny fresh start, so to speak, to talk to her before all my baggage comes with me."

"And knowing Lilli's curiosity, that's all you'll get," Pops added, "a *tiny* start."

"She sounds intriguing," Chris said. "And you say she inherited David's artistic talent?"

"Yes, definitely," Chloe said.

"Could I see some of her work?"

"Of course," Chloe replied. "Shall we go up to her hopefully clean bedroom?"

In Lilli's room, Chris sat on the bed and went through Lilli's drawings, examining each one minutely. When she finished, she looked at Chloe and Pops, who were sitting next to her on the bed.

"This is extraordinary work for an 8-year-old child. Lilli is, without a doubt, gifted. Has she been taking any art lessons?"

"Yes," breathed Chloe. "There is a retired artist in

Pentwater who gives Lilli lessons once a week, though I'm not sure she always appreciates them."

"No doubt she has her own ideas. Artists are notoriously individualistic and stubborn at times. When you create you must know your own mind. But Lilli, with this kind of talent, should have instruction in technique and different mediums. It's important for artists to work in all mediums, because they tend to focus on one or two later in their career. It aids them immeasurably to be forced at the beginning to use water colors, oils, pencils, chalk—a whole group of instruments, not just those they feel most comfortable with. Perhaps a younger, more dynamic teacher would be in order."

"Not likely available in Pentwater except in the summer on vacation, like David was," Chloe blurted out. Her face suddenly flushed as she realized what she had said. But Chris was oblivious to everything except Lilli's work.

"Remarkable, remarkable," she murmured. "You're absolutely right. She has inherited David's talent; a large measure of it, I'd say, from her work. She'll definitely need lessons while she is in Chicago with us."

Chloe gulped and glanced at Pops, who, like her, was close to tears. This sounded good.

"I hope we haven't hindered her development," Chloe said. "But there isn't much to offer in art lessons here in Pentwater."

"No, no. I realize that. Talent like Lilli's would grow if she never had a lesson. And I can see she has studied from some of her techniques. But it may be that we can continue the good work you've begun."

"Might even David ..."

Chris laughed. "No, no, dear. David is no teacher. He'll have to be restrained from influencing her work. We had a great deal of trouble with him when our daughter began art lessons. But with such talent as this—no." She laughed again. "He has to be restrained, as good as his intentions are. Technique is something you can teach, but style is every artist's individual accomplishment. And, as I said, David is no teacher, of either technique or style. Teaching, I'm afraid, is a separate gift. A lesser artist can be a great teacher and vice versa, as is certainly the case with my husband."

Chloe was amazed. Chris Trassault knew her art. She saw a new world opening for Lilli, a world of art galleries and talking to famous artists—even David was well-known—and careful stimulus of her talent by excellent lessons. Lilli, she knew, lived and breathed art. How she would love it, and what good it would do her. But Chloe had a few questions.

"Isn't Lilli a little young for such serious study? I mean, she is just like every other 8-year-old girl except for art. She is a good student. But no teacher has called her gifted in any other subject."

"I'm thinking—and correct me if I am wrong—the only times that Lilli will be able to visit us are holidays from school and summer vacation. She will remain in Pentwater for the school year. Does that sound logical to you?"

"Yes," Pops said with a sigh, the muscles in his face relaxing. "Oh, yes." Chloe thought how much that comment meant to Pops—and to Chloe. Except now she might be moving to Chicago.

"Before Lilli comes home from school, I want to discuss a difficult subject, difficult for all of us. I want to talk about how this precious child came to be and the role my husband played. As I mentioned to you before, Chloe, this is not the first time, nor was it the last, that my husband strayed in our marriage."

"I'm so sorry," is all Chloe could think of to say.

"Thank you," Chris said. "It has been the severest test of our marriage, to get past David's infidelity. David, I believe, finally realizes how much pain he has caused his family and others. Your own family is a perfect example."

"Definitely," Pops agreed, "a great deal of damage."

"As I understand it, Marie was only 20 the summer she and David became involved. And David has more regrets about Marie because of her youth and innocence and the fact that she died soon after giving birth to his child."

"As he should," Pops exclaimed.

"As he should. I can only imagine the bitterness you must have felt towards David and why you thought it best to keep Marie's promise to exclude him from Lilli's life."

"Until now," Pops remarked.

"Until now. Hopefully we are at a the beginning of a blending of two families with Lilli the tie that connects us all."

"That's right. It's Lilli," Pops said. "That poor little girl has no mother and no father in her life. No child should have to endure that if her father exists."

"And he does, he does, chastened and properly put down by his former actions, we can all hope."

"Yes, let's hope so," Pops said.

"My husband's 'appetites,' I believe, have slowed in recent years, though I can't say I trust him completely. But that, again, is my problem, and an old one, I'm afraid."

"You deserve better," Pops blurted out. Chloe could see he was impressed by Chris Trassault's calm, reasonable manner when discussing her husband's dalliances.

Chris nodded her head slightly.

"Thank you. Many marriages could not survive this. But what I want you to know is that my husband is, despite this severe flaw in his character, a very loving, caring, interesting person. He is a remarkable man. Otherwise I'm sure I would have left him long ago. I'm saying this because I want to assure you Lilli *will* benefit from knowing her father and our household runs on a higher moral plane than what my husband has shown you."

"We had hoped for that," Pops said.

"You were right to contact him. I want you to know I am ready to look at Lilli as my daughter too. The fact is, I would enjoy having a child around the house again. I miss my children. And I believe that, through my work on the Arts Council and being around artists, I could help her expand and grow her talent. I guess what I'm trying to say is, 'Trust us. We'll treat Lilli well.' But, there again, time will bear that out."

"We need to get to know one another," Chloe said.

"Yes," Chris agreed. "That's why I wanted this time before Lilli came home, to get to know one other and discuss our mutual goals for Lilli. And I'd like to learn more about the Hening family. Feel free to ask me any questions you have about myself, David or our children. We will be sharing the life of a child, a very important child to all of us. We need continuity."

"I couldn't agree more," Pops said.

"Let me take you out to lunch," Chris said. "Then we can talk. And perhaps you can show me around this beautiful place and tell me a little about Lilli's life and yours."

Lunch passed swiftly, as did the early afternoon. Chloe felt the way she did at family reunions, getting to know your extended family better. It was a special time which left her—and she was sure Pops—feeling more and more relieved about Lilli. They were adding to their family instead of inviting more conflict into their life.

But 3:30 p.m. and Lilli's arrival was quickly approaching when Chris said, "It was hard to restrain David from jumping on the plane with me. He is eager to see Lilli himself, to be a Daddy to her. What do you think of the first weekend in December as a time for David and I to come?"

"I'm glad it's soon," Chloe said. "Once Lilli knows about David, she will be wild to deal with until she sees him. She's missed having a father for so long."

"Well, we're having our son and daughter home on Thanksgiving, a family time to mend and restore bonds. And we'll show them Lilli's pictures. Then David and I will come to Pentwater. Do you think Lilli would enjoy a letter from David and some pictures of her new family?"

"Do I?" Pops exclaimed. "No question about it. And she'll respond; pages and pages, I imagine."

"It's a good way to get her emotions ready to meet David," Chris added. "She is so young."

Chloe couldn't help giving Chris a hug.

"You're amazing, Chris. David is lucky to have you in his life."

"And for my part," Chris said, hugging Chloe—and Pops—in return, "I'm delighted to find you such warm, wonderful people. It makes me even more excited to see Lilli."

Pops glanced out the window. "You won't have to wait long. Here she comes."

The door opened. Lilli burst in and flung her books down.

"Chloe, I'm ..."

She stopped when she saw the strange woman standing in the entryway with grandpa and her aunt.

"Lilli," Chloe said, "you remember I told you a lady was coming today? Well, this is Chris."

Lilli solemnly held out her hand. Chloe knew Lilli was hungry and bursting with school news. But she was glad she remembered her manners.

"Hello, Lilli," Chris began. "I've heard so much about you from your grandpa and aunt. I'm glad to finally meet you."

"Me too," Lilli said politely. She squirmed slightly and looked at Chloe as though to say, "Who is this woman, anyway?"

"Your grandfather and aunt have shown me some of your artwork. It's very good. Do you like to draw, Lilli?"

"Yes," Lilli said emphatically, "more than anything."

"Well, I come from Chicago. And I know some artists. And I think ..."

"Do you know my dad? He's an artist. His name is David. My grandpa and Chloe are trying to find him for me."

Pops looked at his watch. "Less than two minutes," he said, with a fond smile for Lilli.

Chris Trassault took a deep breath.

"Well, Lilli, you've come right to the point."

"Do you know my father?"

"Yes," Chris said. "I know your father very well."

"Oh," Lilli cried, clapping her hands together loudly. "Can you tell me where he lives?"

"In Chicago, honey," Chloe interposed gently. "That's the surprise. We've found your father."

Lilli stood there silent, her mouth a round "o" with one hand on each cheek. She seemed too dumbfounded to speak. But that only lasted a second. Then the torrent of words began.

"When did you find him? Why didn't you tell me sooner? Does he know about me? Why doesn't he come to see me?"

She turned to Chris Trassault.

"*You* live in Chicago. Can you take me to Chicago to meet my father?"

"Slow down, sweetheart, and listen to Chris," Chloe said, putting her arm around Lilli's shoulders. "She has more to tell you."

"I'm so excited," Lilli gasped, clamping her hand over her mouth in an attempt, it seemed, to silence herself. Then she sat primly on the floor. "I'm listening," she said, wide brown eyes gazing upward at Chris.

Chloe could see Chris swallowing hard, trying not to cry. *It must be hard on her*, Chloe thought, *with this little reincarnation of David sitting in front of her.* Pops was similarly affected. And Chloe was growing misty herself. But Chris regained control and began.

"Your grandpa and Chloe found your father's address in Chicago. They wrote him a letter telling him about you. Your father hadn't known about you until then, or he would have come looking for you."

"How do you know my father?" Lilli asked.

"I'm his wife."

"His wife?" Lilli said incredulously. "But my mother ..."

Chloe was impressed with how Chris sidestepped *that* issue. Chris continued gently, "You're the only child your father and mother have. But you have a brother and a sister who are also your father's children and have *me* as their mother. They're older than you, but would love to see you. Would you like to see pictures of them?"

"I don't understand. Why ..." Then Lilli stopped, digesting the incredible fact she no longer was an only child. "*Of course* I want to see them. Do they look like me?"

"Elaine does, quite a bit. But I think Joseph looks more like his mother, me."

"Everybody thinks I look like my dad."

"Oh, you do; you do. Would you like to see pictures of him too?"

"Yes, oh, yes. I have some pictures of my father I could show you too."

"Go get them, Lilli. We'll look at them together."

As Lilli dashed upstairs, Chris whispered to Chloe, "Good grief. She is razor-sharp. But we'll wait to answer a few of those questions."

Chloe patted Chris on the shoulder.

"You did fine; a born politician."

"An extremely nervous one."

An hour later, Chloe felt her life at Manitou Inn was transformed. Lilli, snuggled up next to Chris Trassault, was poring over several albums Chris had brought of David, she and the kids. Pops and Chloe leaned over their shoulders to get a look too. Chris even showed

Lilli pictures of David's parents and her own.

"Now, besides grandpa, I have *four* more grandparents. Isn't that the best, Chloe?"

Lilli did not go to bed until 11:00 p.m. that evening.

"I can't sleep yet," she insisted.

She spent the hours asking Chris endless questions.

Chloe could see Chris' demeanor toward Lilli grow from cautious kindness to warm affection. Chris became more spirited and relaxed, softly stroking Lilli's dark hair as Lilli leaned against her shoulder looking at pictures. Because Lilli pleaded with her to stay, Chris changed her Tuesday flight to Wednesday morning.

"I'll miss you at school tomorrow. Chloe, can I stay home?"

"No, darling. You have to go to school."

"But you'll be here when I come home?" Lilli asked.

"Yes, dear," Chris answered, caught up in Lilli's excitement. "How would you like to talk to your father on the phone tomorrow?"

"I would," Lilli cried, jumping up and down. "This is the best day of my life!"

Though she protested she would *never* sleep, Lilli fell into a deep slumber as soon as her head touched the pillow.

After Chris talked to David for over an hour Tuesday morning, Chloe and Pops took her on a walk through Pentwater and showed her every nook and cranny of Manitou Inn. Chris seemed interested in all she saw. And afterwards, when Pops ambled off to fetch Charlie to repaint a stained wall, Chris suggested a walk on the beach.

"You certainly know my number," Chloe said with a laugh. "Or has Pops told you I'm a beach fanatic?"

"No," Chris replied. "I'm an outdoor person. I love to ramble. And here you have the perfect place to walk."

"But today is coat weather."

"I've brought my outdoor jacket. Chicago is not the

tropics, you know," Chris reminded her.

"You're on," Chloe said. And, after bundling up, they set off.

The winds were gusty and the air raw. Breakers rumbled on the lake's shore, and the sky was a leaden gray. The beach was deserted except for a solitary man walking his dog. Chloe breathed in deeply, filling her lungs with cold, crisp air. She loved Pentwater at these times, isolated and majestic with a power not found in summer.

"You're lucky to live here," Chris said quietly.

"I love it," Chloe agreed. "But I may soon have to leave."

Chris looked startled. "Whatever for?"

"I'm going to be married."

"Oh, I see. And your fiancé doesn't live in Pentwater?"

"No," Chloe said, sighing. "He lives in Chicago."

"What a huge change for you," Chris murmured. "You'll miss your father and Lilli."

"Yes. There are times I don't think I can endure it."

"I understand. Yet Chicago can be a thrilling place to live with all its diversity; museums, theaters, the arts."

"I'm a simple person, I'm afraid. All that means nothing to me next to walking along the beach like this."

Chris looked around her. "It *does* turn everything else into specks of dust, doesn't it? And, this fiancé of yours, what does he do?"

"He spearheads renovations of individual hotels like Manitou Inn, incorporating them into his father's hotel chain. That's how I met him. Manitou Inn is undergoing a renovation and is now partially owned by his father."

"I see," Chris said. She looked as if she wanted to say more but, thinking the better of it, remained silent.

Chloe, to her own amazement, was close to tears.

"I just don't think he understands."

"Understands what, dear?"

This term of endearment touched Chloe, and she swallowed hard, trying not to sob.

"How much this," she said, gesturing around her, "means to me and how I hate to leave my family. He doesn't even understand how I feel about God."

"You've told him your concerns, Chloe?" Chris asked, slipping her arm around Chloe's shoulder.

"I have. But he's so … impetuous, I guess, is the word. He pushes my worries aside. He thinks love will make everything work out. I've known him a little over two months. There is so much about each other we don't understand. Oh, Chris, what have I gotten myself into?"

"And you've just become engaged?"

"Yes," Chloe said, sniffling.

"Don't let anybody pressure you into marriage, Chloe," Chris said emphatically, "especially if he doesn't share your love of the Lord. I'm the perfect example. When I married David, I was in love. I thought I could change him; tame him, if you will. I was young and naïve enough to think he would soon believe as I did. David's lack of faith allowed him to give in to temptations, which caused our family and others such pain. As he grows older, David shows signs of change. He attends church with me now. Take your time, Chloe, until you are sure where your relationship is headed. It will save you trouble later. Marriage is for life. And a poor marriage is like carrying a large rock on your back, one you will never be free of."

Chloe brushed at her tears with her jacket sleeve and hugged Chris. It was good to talk to someone who understood what she was going through. And Chris did understand.

"Thank you, Chris. You see my dilemma. Even Pops and Lilli don't understand. They're excited for the wedding and …"

"A child and an older man. What do they understand? It's *your* life, Chloe, and your decision.

Even your fiancé can't make up your mind for you. Don't let him."

"Okay," Chloe said, managing a small smile. "I won't."

Chris put both hands on Chloe's arms and looked at her seriously.

"Promise me you won't marry until you have settled these doubts in your mind."

"I promise," Chloe said.

"I'm anxious to meet this young man."

"You will. You will soon."

That evening was a special one, with Lilli's first phone call to her father. Lilli insisted upon calling the number herself—Chloe wondered at her boldness in such a situation—and said in a lilting voice, "Hello? Father? This is Lilli, your daughter." This had Chloe and Chris both in tears and Pops holding his back with an effort. Lilli's first conversation with her father was a voluble one. Both parties had a lot to say. It lasted over an hour. Chloe had a hard time prying the phone out of Lilli's hands. This only happened with the promise of another call *tomorrow night* to both David and Chris.

Before she went to bed, Lilli ran into Chris' arms and kissed her on her cheek.

"Oh, thank you, Chris, for letting me call my father. I love you."

"I love you too, sweetie," Chris said, obviously touched.

When Chris left the next morning, Chloe felt a familiar isolation. With Chris Chloe could talk about her innermost feelings, and it was a great release. It made her miss her own mother. Chloe realized she shared a bond with this unique woman who had quickly woven her way into their lives.

16 CHICAGO VISIT

After Chris left Tuesday morning, Chloe had only a few days to catch up on her accounts and hotel duties before Braden made his appearance Friday night and took up her whole weekend. There was the joy Tuesday night of watching—and listening—to Lilli talk to her father for the second time. Chloe and Pops loved to see the glow on Lilli's face, her excited gesturing and her rapid-fire happy chatter. It was amazing. Father and daughter talked for an hour and, after Lilli hung up the phone, she regaled Pops and Chloe with stories about David, who she now called "Daddy."

"If ever a girl was ready for a father, it's Lilli," Chloe whispered to Pops after tucking Lilli in bed.

Pops grinned. "We *all* need a father, Chloe. I was thinking about the wonderful father we share, our Father in heaven. He has definitely blessed us in this matter."

"A rainbow after the storm," Chloe murmured, hugging him. "It was a long time coming. But now we're in a happy place."

All three members of the Hening family; Chloe, Pops and especially Lilli; walked on clouds these days. Lilli now talked to David nightly—and Chris on occasion too. More surprisingly, David's children called Lilli. Won over by Lilli's eager plunge into the little sister role, their calls became regular and frequent. Lilli dove into these relationships without hesitation. The phone was important to Lilli these days. She asked if she had gotten any calls when she got home from school or after playing with Melanie.

On Thursday night, Chloe had an important call too. It was from Braden's parents. Braden told them about their engagement. Both mother and father were on the line to "welcome Chloe into the family." They *did* sound less frosty than on Chloe's first trip to Chicago. There was a warmth in their regal demeanor, some small letting go of convention, which reassured Chloe.

"We were becoming convinced Braden would remain single," Braden's mother exclaimed. "He's had many young women interested in him, but never a serious relationship—until now, that is. How have you managed it, my dear?"

"I have no idea," Chloe admitted.

"He's a changed man," Braden's father chimed in, "and high time, I'd say. I understand you two will be house hunting in Chicago?"

"I ... I guess," Chloe replied. This was Braden again, pushing the limits, house hunting when they hadn't even set a date for the wedding.

"Braden tells me your niece, Lilli, may be spending time in Chicago visiting her father," Mr. Willis continued.

"That's right," Chloe said.

"She has a talent in art?"

"Yes," Chloe responded, "probably inherited from her father."

"And her father is David Trassault?"

"That's right."

"He is well known in Chicago," Mrs. Willis added, "a gifted artist. We've seen many of his shows."

"Yes," Mr. Willis said. "We're eager to meet Lilli—and

your father, of course."

"We hope you will be able to join us for Thanksgiving dinner this year now that our families will be united," Mrs. Willis said. "Braden's friend, who flew you down for your first visit, will be happy to pick you three up, fly you to Chicago and bring you home to the Ludington airport."

"You're so kind," Chloe said. "But we couldn't let him do that."

"Oh, no problem. He loves to fly and is always looking for an excuse. We've already talked to him about it. It's all been arranged."

"Thank you for the invitation," Chloe said sincerely. "But I'll have to check with my father and ..."

"Oh, by all means, check with your father and get back with us in a couple days."

"I will," Chloe said.

"With our son in the excitable state he is about your upcoming wedding," Mrs. Willis continued, "we'll no doubt know within minutes after he hears anything from you."

"But I'll call you myself," Chloe promised.

"Thank you, my dear. It is good to talk with you. Hopefully we'll see you on Thanksgiving. And we're happy to welcome you as a part of our family. Goodbye now."

Chloe was thoughtful as she hung up the phone. Braden's parents seemed, on the surface at least, to be accepting of their son marrying her. She couldn't help wondering if they were just accepting an unwelcome reality. But she was happy they were hospitable and gracious to her. Chloe's emotions running high lately, and she appreciated their kindness and positive attitude, for whatever reason.

Maybe they won't be difficult to deal with after all, she thought to herself. At least she hoped not. She immediately ran downstairs to find Pops and tell him the news.

"Chicago for Thanksgiving, eh?" Pops said. "Well, why not? Lilli will love the airplane ride. We shouldn't mention it's the city her father lives in, or she'll be dragging us through the streets to find him."

Chloe chuckled. "And that's no exaggeration. I hope you'll like Braden's parents, Pops. They live a life quite different from ours."

"I can imagine."

"It's going to take a lot of getting used to," Chloe said with a sigh, "*my* upcoming change of life, I mean."

Pops peered into her face intently.

"Chloe, you don't seem comfortable with this engagement. Don't let Braden pressure you into anything you don't want or aren't ready for."

"But as you've already said, there are no obstacles to us being married."

"I meant no *outside* obstacles, Chloe. The most important obstacles to this marriage may come from your head and your heart. I've seen Braden with you. It's obvious he has made up his mind. Don't let him make up your mind."

"I won't," Chloe said slowly. "I want to go slower with our relationship than he does, spend more time together before making such a monumental decision."

"That's perfectly reasonable," Pops said.

"Braden doesn't think so. He says he doesn't want to be apart during the week and have to keep coming here on the weekends."

"Then maybe you could alternate," Pops said. "You go to Chicago one weekend and he comes up here the next."

"That's a good thought. I've made him promise no wedding for at least two months. He says he won't wait a day more than six."

"Then I would go for five months at least, to give you more time, Chloe. Marriage is forever. At least that's what God intended. Five months is not a long time when you consider what is at stake."

"Thanks, Pops," Chloe said. "I needed to hear that. You seemed so happy to see me engaged I was afraid you were trying to get rid of me."

Pops chuckled. "No, dear. If you leave for Chicago, I'll miss you a lot."

"And I'll miss you, though Braden says I can visit anytime. He wants to build us a house here."

"That's generous of him," Pops said. "No doubt he can afford to. However, the decision is still yours. Don't let him forget it."

Chloe hugged Pops. "You know what? I'm glad you're my father."

"And I'm glad you're my daughter. I'd be lost without you, Chloe. What would I have done without you all these years? Now I want to see you happy. By the way," Pops continued nonchalantly, "what did Mark Lockley have to say the other night?"

"Can't you imagine?" Chloe retorted, unwilling to get into it.

"I can. And I suppose you told him off?"

"I did."

"Then that's that," Pops said with a small smile. Chloe wished she knew what Pops was thinking. But she didn't want to talk about Mark.

I must bury him in my mind, she thought, *and try to forget him once and for all.*

When Braden came on Friday, Lilli, who was bursting with excitement, flooded him with "facts" about her new family.

"My dad is coming to see me after Thanksgiving. I'm going to have art lessons. I have a new brother and sister. They call me all the time. We .." Then Braden added enchantments Lilli would experience in he and Chloe's household. This made Lilli basically intolerable to Melanie, who left for home early, unable to stand one more minute of her friend's enthusiasm for something Melanie had no part in.

Chloe excused Lilli with, *I don't think she will continue this long. She'll settle down in time.* Chloe was feeling joyful too, delighted with her niece's current happiness. And Lilli wasn't the only one overflowing with exhilaration. Braden, always keyed up, was particularly jubilant this weekend. She hated to put a wet blanket on his enthusiasm. But he was already into house hunting and wedding details, having accomplished the meeting of their two families on Thanksgiving. Chloe, standing in front of him, gently slapped both his cheeks with her hands to get his attention.

"Braden, Braden, slow down. We're going to get there."

"But it's hard to find land around Chicago. I want to build a house on Lake Michigan. I promised you that."

"And you promised me we'd go slow. Why don't we just enjoy ourselves this weekend without worrying about all this stuff?"

"But I enjoy planning our life together, our wedding, our home."

"Can we just stay on the weekend after next, Thanksgiving, when we're coming to Chicago? I'm wondering. Should we get a hotel?"

"Are you kidding? My parents have enough rooms in that house to accommodate a small army."

Chloe laughed. "But, seriously, Braden, you have to make sure it's okay. And what about dinner? Should we bring something?"

"Chloe, get real. My parents won't be doing any of the cooking; their cook will. And they have dinner parties all the time. They never expect guests to bring anything."

"Well, I'll bring them candy or flowers or something to thank them for their hospitality. It's so nice of them to have us."

"Chloe, you're family—or almost. You don't need to stand on ceremony."

"But I ..."

"Then get them something," Braden said with a dismissing wave of his hand. "But don't ask me what. They don't need anything."

"I'll think of something," Chloe murmured. She glanced at Braden. He was brimming with news, she could tell. "What?" she asked.

"I've been thinking. If I promised that you could come up to Pentwater at least two days a week, would that make you happier so we can get going on this wedding? I'm sure you could stay at Manitou Inn until we build the new house and ..."

Chloe had to reach up to kiss Braden on the lips.

"You are so sweet," she said, "to offer me that. But I thought you said you didn't like separations. That would be two days a week."

"Whoa, girl, don't get the wrong idea. I plan to come with you on most of these jaunts. And we can plan some times when *I'll* be out of town on business. So, you see, you can have Pentwater and me too."

"You're a darling, Braden," Chloe said, throwing her arms around his neck and kissing him again. "You're so good to me."

Braden pulled her close. "I just want to make you happy, honey. And I'll try not to push the wedding thing, though I dearly want to marry you very soon. Promise me you won't wait a day longer than you think is necessary."

How else could Chloe respond? She was moved by his concern for her feelings. "I won't. I just need some time to sort things out in my own mind. It's such a big life change. And now with Lilli ..."

"I know, I know. Just don't wait too long, or I'll think you don't love me like I love you. And that *would* be a problem." Braden suddenly looked somber. "Love has to be a two-way street to work, Chloe. And if you're unsure of your love for me, you should tell me. I can take it."

Chloe involuntarily shivered and looked away from

him. "Oh, Braden, you know I care about you. A thousand other girls would just say 'yes' and marry you immediately. But I take marriage seriously and ..."

Braden drew her close and hugged her tightly.

"Chloe, I'm sorry. I guess I am impetuous about this. I'll try to go easy on you for awhile; I said *try*. I guess I can understand leaving a small town for a big city can be frightening; the change, that is."

"And I've been happy here," Chloe said wistfully.

"Like I said, I'll try to tone it down, but no guarantees. You may have to hit me over the head a few times."

"Which I'll do gladly," Chloe said with a laugh, "only if you promise not to hit me back."

Lilli was enthralled with her private airplane ride to Chicago. With her nose pressed tight against the window, she exclaimed, "Look, those are clouds beneath us. There's the lake. Where are we now? I see tiny cars."

Chloe tried to respond to Lilli's comments and questions quickly so she wouldn't distract their pilot with her constant chatter. When Chloe, Pops and Lilli hopped out of Braden's friend's lightweight plane at the private airstrip used by the members of this exclusive suburban complex outside Chicago, they looked around in amazement. Everything was big and close together.

How am I ever going to get used to this? Chloe thought.

"Come on, folks," said Braden's friend, their pilot. "I see your 'limo' now."

Limo is right, Chloe thought, for up pulled a long and lovely beige Mercedes. Before it stopped completely, Braden emerged and sprinted towards them. He gave Chloe a kiss, Lilli a hug and shook hands with Pops.

"I'm *so* glad to see you. Mr. Hening and Lilli, you've never met my parents," he said, gesturing towards his mom and dad, who were just getting out of the car. As they approached, Mr. Willis stepped forward and shook

Pops' hand heartily.

"Glad to meet you. It looks like a wedding is soon going to make us family."

"Yes, it does," Pops said with a serene smile. "And we want to thank you for including us in your Thanksgiving celebration."

"We're delighted," Mr. Willis said with a smile.

Mrs. Willis also greeted Pops and shook his hand. But it was Lilli she was staring at with delight.

"So this is your darling Lilli!" she exclaimed to Pops, softly patting Lilli's head.

"Yes," Pops said, and his smile grew brighter.

"She is adorable. And you're right. She *does* resemble her father."

"My father? Do you know him?" Lilli asked eagerly.

Chloe wished Braden's mother had not brought up David. Before they left for Chicago, Pops and Chloe reminded Lilli she would *not* be seeing her father on this trip. And after days of explaining why she would have to wait to see David, Chloe was afraid any mention of her father would quicken Lilli's excitement to a fever pitch.

Chloe handed Mrs. Willis her hostess gift, a framed watercolor Lilli had painted of Edgar, their cat. Mrs. Willis studied the painting carefully, pursing her lips.

"You have a wonderful talent, Lilli," she enthused.

"Oh, I dunno ..." Lilli began.

Lilli was *always* delighted to talk about art, about her pictures. But she would rather discuss what was good or bad in them, what she could have done differently, better. Lilli was clearly uncomfortable with overt praise.

"You'll simply *have* to meet some of my more artistic friends," Mrs. Willis gushed. "Won't they be amazed, Jim?"

Braden's father nodded in agreement.

"You have a real little protégée there," he said to Pops.

"How proud you must be of Lilli's accomplishments," Mrs. Willis added.

"We are," Chloe said.

"Come on, you guys," Braden said impatiently. "Let's get back to the house. It's cold out here."

Pops' eyes widened when he saw the size and grandeur of Braden's parents' house rising majestically at the end of a tree-lined driveway, its white siding and wraparound porch giving it the look of a Southern mansion.

"They can't need all *this* room," he muttered to Chloe as they stood in the entryway waiting to be dispatched to their rooms.

After a "simple" meal of tiny sandwiches, fruit, juice and desert delivered to their rooms by a maid in a crisp uniform, Pops kissed Chloe and Lilli goodnight and returned to his room, saying the plane ride had "wore him out." Lilli, however, who shared Chloe's room, was wide awake, excitedly darting about and admiring her new surroundings.

"Oo, Chloe, come see these bars of soap. They're shaped like seashells. Look, Chloe, the chairs, bedspread and curtains all match. *I* want a room like this. Can I, Chloe?"

Chloe smiled. "We'll see, honey." Then the phone rang. When Chloe answered, it was Braden.

"When can I see you? Is Lilli sleeping yet?"

"Oh, Braden," Chloe said, laughing, "what you know about kids is not a lot. But I'll tell you what might satisfy our little rascal," she said, giving Lilli a wink, "a tour of your beautiful home. *Then* I may be able to get her into bed."

So Braden obligingly escorted them around the house, all three floors of it, while Lilli softly touched china figurines, rolled on squishy carpets and oohed and aahed over chandeliers, plush furniture and, most of all, the gorgeous paintings adorning the walls.

"Braden, did my father paint any of these?" Lilli

whispered, her father never far from her thoughts.

"I don't know," Braden answered truthfully. "Ask my mother tomorrow."

"I will," Lilli said, sighing.

"And now to bed, buttercup," Chloe said. "You've had your tour."

They sat with Lilli until she fell asleep. Then Braden motioned for Chloe to follow him. Just outside the bedroom door he pulled her close. "Now I get *my* bedtime kiss."

Chloe pulled away after a brief kiss, leaning on the bedroom door. "Braden, not here."

Braden sighed. "I can tell this is going to be a long weekend of not seeing you alone."

"But what did you expect?"

"This," Braden said, kissing her again.

Chloe grasped the door handle.

"This is not going to happen when we're married," Braden said, pouting.

"You're right," Chloe responded. "But 'til then"—she kissed him gently on the cheek—"goodnight."

The next morning began early for Chloe. She opened her eyes to find Lilli behind the heavy drapery they had drawn the night before.

"Lilli, what are you doing?" she asked sleepily.

Lilli's head peeked out from behind the brocade folds of fabric.

"Chloe, you won't believe this. There are horses in a field right by the house."

"They're Braden's mom and dad's," Chloe said. "Didn't I tell you they had horses?"

"I don't know. I forget. But can I ride one?"

"Maybe a pony, if they have one," Chloe said. "These horses aren't used to being ridden." This statement wasn't entirely true. She and Braden had ridden on their last visit. That jolting ride and the resulting stiffness made Chloe less than eager to try it again or have Lilli unnecessarily endanger herself. Chloe wanted to avoid the horses. She gently tried to dissuade Lilli, but with little success. Lilli was still at it during breakfast.

"Braden, can I ride a horse? Please?"

Braden looked mock serious. "Are you a better rider than your Aunt Chloe?"

Chloe, sitting next to him, swatted Braden's arm.

"Why, Chloe," Braden's mother said, "did Braden take you with him on one of his wild gallops through the field the last time you were here?"

"Yes."

Mr. Willis shook his finger at Braden. "No more of that, young man. She could have fallen."

Braden laughed out loud. "Don't worry, father. *Nothing* was going to separate Chloe from that horse. I had to pry her hands from the saddle horn just to get her off."

"You poor dear," Mrs. Willis said, then turned to Lilli.

"No one but Braden rides those horses, Lilli. And he's too busy to do it often." But she softened when she saw Lilli's excitement. "How about if Braden held the reins and walked you around the paddock? Would that make you happy?"

"Oh, yes," Lilli said dreamily. "That would be great."

So there was no question of how the morning hours would be spent. After breakfast, Pops, Chloe, Lilli and Braden went down to the stables. The gentlest horse was saddled for Lilli. Braden was patient, walking Lilli around and around the paddock. Pops took pictures. ("To show Melanie," Lilli said.) It was 12:30 p.m. before they knew it. Braden's father appeared, asking if they wanted to "freshen up" before dinner at 2:00 p.m.

They returned to the house, showered to remove the smell of horse and dressed in the Thanksgiving finery they had brought.

"A princess might live like this," Lilli exclaimed as

Chloe brushed her long dark hair and pulled it back from her face with two ribbons. "I'm having fun."

But Lilli's fun ended at dinner. Braden's parents invited five other couples their age who were dressed to the hilt—not a child in sight—to share Thanksgiving dinner with them. The table was elegantly set and the turkey and ham looked picture perfect, too pretty almost to cut into. *Everything* was perfect. But it wasn't home and it wasn't fun. You had to find the right silverware from an amazing glittering array and make polite conversation and not spill anything. Chloe could see it was stifling Lilli, who looked serious and only picked at her food.

Braden's mother took delight in informing her guests Lilli was David Trassault's daughter. She showed them Lilli's picture, hanging prominently on a wall in the dining area. Her guests, duly impressed, asked Lilli questions. Lilli answered them in a small voice or with a solemn nod of her head.

Braden, oblivious to the Henings' struggles, engaged the men, who it appeared he knew from his father's business, in discussions of recent acquisitions, deals and shop small talk. It appeared to Chloe Braden was in his element, while she ... she glanced at Pops, who shrugged slightly. Pops tolerated situations like this well. It was part of his job to get along with people, and he dealt with many wealthy Chicagoans at Manitou Inn.

After never-ending courses of rich food, everyone had after-dinner drinks in the lounge. Then the couples left. Mr. and Mrs. Willis quickly released the Hennings to their rooms for the evening. Chloe caught Pops' eye over Lilli's sleepy head.

"Lots of pomp and ceremony, not enough holiday," Pops murmured. Chloe nodded.

After slipping off Lilli's party dress and tucking her under the covers, Chloe heard a soft knock on the door. She opened it a crack to find Braden, flushed from his after-dinner cocktails, smiling at her.

"I have to make sure Lilli's asleep," she whispered.

"Meet me downstairs," he whispered back. "I'll be in the living room."

Chloe closed the door gently and sat on the bed next to Lilli, softly stroking some straying locks of dark hair. From Lilli's soft, shallow breathing, Chloe could tell her niece was already asleep. But Chloe needed to collect her thoughts for a moment.

This is how I'll spend the holidays, she thought. *I'll be the "other" Mrs. Willis. Braden will expect me to entertain his friends and blend into his lifestyle.* A tear slipped from the corner of her eye, which she quickly brushed away. She tried to collect herself. *I have to remember Braden's kindness and how he loves me. He promised me weekly trips to Pentwater, a house there. Things will work out. I'll be fine. Most people would kill for this kind of life.* But she knew in her heart she was *not* "most people."

Finally she could bear her thoughts no longer. She softly kissed Lilli's cheek, tiptoed out of the door and ran down the stairs to Braden's embrace.

17 A MEETING AND WEDDING PLANS

Back in Pentwater Sunday night, Pops, Chloe and Lilli had little to say to each other about their Thanksgiving in Chicago. Lilli was enthralled on the airplane ride home, delighting in the sun sinking red and gold into Lake Michigan and the many twinkling lights of the towns she saw beneath her. Chloe had to agree it was a wonderful sight. But the weekend cast a pall over the Henings. It simply hadn't seemed like Thanksgiving. Pops looked thoughtful. And Chloe had difficulty sounding joyful when Braden called that night, filled with how well everything went. She was sincere when she asked him to thank his parents again. They had been all graciousness with none of the shadow of her first visit. But Chloe found herself actually rubbing the pillowcase gently with her cheek and murmuring, "I'm home. I'm home." She didn't want to think about what that meant. She merely fell asleep and awoke happy to be in her own bed Monday morning. The bright morning sun filtered through her curtain, and a stiff, cold wind rattled the windowpanes.

It was comforting to settle back into her accounts and the bustle of Manitou Inn, though now it was more the workers sawing and painting the rooms. They had few guests in November and December. Business would pick up slightly for snowboarding and skiing and blossom like flowers in spring. The renovation was in full swing, and Pops and Chloe were caught up in it.

On Wednesday night, Chris and David Trassault called to remind them they would be arriving Saturday morning. But no reminder was needed.

"Lilli asks every other minute how many days until you come," Chloe told Chris after Lilli and David had chatted awhile.

"David is getting nervous," Chris admitted in a soft voice.

"Why?" Chloe asked, suddenly fearful.

"I think facing you and your father scares him a bit."

"Reassure him, then," Chloe begged. "We are so happy, after all our troubles, to have this day finally arrive."

"I'll tell him that," Chris said. "He's excited and happy—don't misunderstand—just grasping the enormity of it, I guess. He's afraid Lilli will be disappointed in him. He wonders how he'll answer her questions."

"But he's already answered thousands over the phone," Chloe reminded her.

"True. But face to face—well, it's got to be difficult at first. But he can't wait to come. You can expect us at 10:00 a.m. Saturday. David wants to have the entire weekend with his daughter."

"And Lilli will welcome him with her whole heart. Her excitement is building and wearing her grandfather and I out."

"'Til Saturday then," Chris said.

Braden arrived early Friday night because, as he said, "As a member of this family, I want to make sure Lilli is surrounded by people who love her." Chloe was nervous herself. She clung to him Friday night, which Braden loved.

"I'm so glad you came."

"You can depend on me," he replied.

"I know. And I need you now," she said, giving him a squeeze and a kiss.

By Saturday morning it was apparent the fear that struck David was now affecting Lilli. She grew quiet and pensive, putting her index finger in her mouth and chewing on it as she had long ago in babyhood. Her wide-spaced brown eyes grew enormous, and she flushed and paled so Chloe was afraid she was going to faint.

Chloe thought of what Chris said about preparing Lilli. Now she could see what she meant. Lilli ran up to Chloe and threw her arms around her waist, hiding her head in Chloe's stomach. She mumbled something.

"What honey?"

"What ... what if he ... doesn't like me?"

"Oh, honey," Chloe said, bending down and trying to look into Lilli's face. "Of course he'll like you. He'll love you. You're very lovable, you know."

"I am?"

"You know you are."

"Okay." Lilli gulped, squaring her little shoulders like a miniature soldier. "I'm ready."

Ten minutes later the doorbell rang. Pops answered it. Chloe remained with Lilli, who was still engulfed by her sudden fear.

Chris and David Trassault entered. Chris had a smile on her face. David held tightly to her arm, looking for all the world ... well, like Lilli, frozen and mute. *He has aged*, Chloe thought, his dark hair graying around the temples and his face lined. What hadn't changed were his eyes, still twinkling with radiant life and as brim full of magic as ever. That he was terrified of this meeting was apparent.

His eyes immediately locked with Lilli's. Father and daughter stared at each other for a long moment. Then they uttered a choked cry and started toward each other, ending in an embrace wet by both their tears.

"Daddy," Lilli cried, totally unglued and acting as though she had known David all her life. "Where have you been? I've missed you."

"Oh, Lilli," David sobbed. "I'm sorry. I'm so sorry. How can I make it up to you?"

"Don't leave me again."

"I won't, my darling. I won't."

By this time Chloe and Chris had tears on their cheeks. Pops was taking large gulping breaths. Even Braden looked moved. Lilli and David just held each other tightly in silence until they were calm enough to look each other in the face and smile.

Then, amazingly, their calm returned.

Lilli said to no one in particular, "I've got a daddy. Now I've got a daddy."

"You sure do, honey," Chloe said.

"Now, Lilli, you have to tell me what you've been doing your whole life without me. I've heard some things over the phone. Now I want the entire story."

Chloe could see David was mock serious. But Lilli took him at his word.

"This is where I live," Lilli exclaimed, twirling like a ballerina and gesturing broadly.

David looked around hesitantly. "It's different than how I remember," he said in a soft voice.

"We're renovating," Braden broke in.

David looked at Pops apprehensively.

"I hope you can find it in your heart to forgive me."

"You have *my* forgiveness," Pops said, beaming. "All it took was the look on Lilli's face when she first saw you."

"But why..." Lilli started.

Pops held up his hand. "Now, Lilli, you heard what your father asked you. Tell him everything."

"Okay," Lilli said, warming to her subject. She grabbed Edgar the cat, who was roaming back and forth, alert to the excitement in the air, and thrust him into David's arms. "This is Edgar, my cat." David held Edgar gently, stroking him behind his ears.

"I can see Edgar is a fine, large cat." He looked at some pictures hanging in the living room. "These paintings are very good. Can you tell me who painted them?"

"I did," Lilli said excitedly. "I've got more in my room. Do you want to see them ... Daddy?"

Chloe could tell Lilli was delighted, though a little hesitant still, to use that wonderful word.

Soon Chris and David were marching up to Lilli's room, where she promised to show them "everything."

"Well," Chloe said wryly to Pops, "since we've already seen 'everything' and Lilli's room is not large enough to hold all of us, I guess you, I and Braden can go on with our lives."

"Sounds like a good idea to me," Pops said and ambled off whistling a tune.

Until the moment late Sunday when David and Chris Trassault closed the front door on their way to the airport, Manitou Inn was full and humming that weekend, punctuated by Lilli's non-stop exuberance and the reflected glow shown by every other member of "her" family.

"We shouldn't wait long to have kids," Braden said wistfully. Braden, though least affected by the reunion of father and daughter, was drawn to the overflowing love fest occurring under his nose.

The more Chloe and Pops knew Chris and David, the more comfortable they felt letting them take Lilli to Chicago from time to time. To everyone's joy and relief, an amazing family feeling was developing.

David presented Lilli with a real artist's set of watercolors, oil paints and charcoal. Then Lilli insisted they set up her easel and have David draw for her. As Pops, Chloe and Braden couldn't stop hovering around,

David drew some simple sketches of them. It became a sort of game, with everyone commenting on how like they were or suggesting changes. Lilli insisted David accompany her to the beach, and the rest of them followed. A shivering yet invigorating football toss began, followed by a sing-a-long next to a glowing fireplace fire that evening. David brought his guitar and put it to good use. Chloe had some blue memories, brought on by remembering that summer with Marie. David knew a store of silly songs and used them to good effect. At the end of Saturday evening, they all had laughed their share and were ready to sleep.

David and Chris called their children during their two days at Manitou Inn, and Lilli talked to them too.

After one of these phone calls, Chris approached Chloe with an excited Lilli in tow. They both started speaking at once, looked at each other and then burst into giggles.

"What's up?" Chloe asked.

"Well, David and I thought, because this is our first Christmas with Lilli, we might come to Manitou Inn so we could all share in the festivities together."

"Wouldn't that be great, Chloe?" Lilli squealed.

Chris laughed. "Of course, this is the ultimate of nerve, inviting ourselves to your home for the holidays. But ..."

"No," Chloe said immediately. "I'm just sorry I hadn't thought of it first. It would be a wonderful tradition to start."

"We want to have all of you down too," Chris said with a laugh. "But since our life with Lilli is just beginning, we thought she would be more comfortable and happy to spend the holidays at Manitou Inn."

"But we want to share them with her," David, who had trailed them into the room, added firmly.

"I understand," Chloe said. "I know I can speak for Pops that he and I will be delighted to have you for Christmas."

"That's not all," Chris admitted sheepishly. "Of course, our son and daughter want to come too. They will be on holiday from school and are anxious to meet their new sister."

Chloe hit her head with her hand. "I'm so dense. Why don't I think of these things?"

Chris gave her a hug.

"You're doing great, honey. You handle everything so well."

Braden put his hand on Chloe's arm, turning her toward him. "Don't forget about me. This is your first Christmas with *me* too. How about inviting my folks down too? They'd love to see Manitou Inn, and you owe them."

"Of course, of course," Chloe said. "And Manitou Inn is the perfect place for such a crowd. We're near empty during the holidays with rooms galore."

Chloe's head was spinning. From their little Christmas celebrations of past years, just she, Pops and Lilli, they were certainly an expanding family.

After David and Chris left, Chloe called Braden's parents, who quickly accepted her offer to come to Manitou Inn at Christmas. *What a weekend this has been,* Chloe thought to herself, finally ready to sleep after bidding Braden goodbye that evening. *And Christmas is only two and a half weeks away.*

The next weekend, ignoring the fact they had not yet set a date for the wedding, Braden was full of plans, plans for their new life together. He was drawing up blueprints, in his mind at least, for a new house in Chicago and one in Pentwater. And he was looking in both places for "the perfect location" to build. But Braden's exuberance and forward thrusting made Chloe nervous.

"Braden, all this with Lilli and David and everyone coming at Christmas, we have to give that first priority now," she begged. "My mind is bursting as it is without deciding how to build two houses. Why, we could live in an apartment for awhile, as far as that goes."

"Are you kidding?" Braden replied. "We've got to have a house—no, two houses—and fantastic ones at that. After all the time I've spent furnishing and rebuilding other people's property, I've got plenty of ideas on how to build a house right."

"Well, great," Chloe said with a sigh. "But I want you to promise me not to put your name on paper until after Christmas, when I can get my act together and concentrate more."

At her response, his brows rushed together in what was becoming a frequent look of frustration. Chloe could see putting a hold on Braden's plans would be more and more difficult.

"Chloe, for heaven sakes, what's all this about Christmas? I'll tell you what. I know people who can take care of Christmas for you—decorators, cleanup squads, caterers. There's no excuse for you doing everything yourself. Hire it done. I'll pay, you know."

"It's not the same. Don't you see that?" Chloe said, trying to make him understand. "Christmas has great meaning to our family. It's our Savior's birth. We've created special traditions. Hiring a caterer wouldn't be the same."

"Of course not. It would be a lot less work," Braden said, looking perturbed. Then he looked at her intently. "Unless you're just stalling on our wedding again."

Chloe, infuriated at his badgering, held her ground.

"You're right. I'm not going to commit to a marriage until we agree on important matters."

Braden's look darkened further.

"You mean religion, don't you? You know I've been going to church with you. And I promised I will after we marry. So what's the problem?"

"But do you *believe*? Do you see the importance of faith? How can we bind our lives together without sharing that?"

"People do every day," Braden answered curtly. "They just don't worry about it like you do."

"Then marry somebody like that," Chloe shot back, "not me."

"Chloe," Braden said softly, relenting and taking her into his arms, "let's not fight. You know it's *you* I want, stubbornness and all."

"I'm not stubborn. I..." Chloe began.

Braden silenced her reply with a kiss and changed the subject.

Chloe and Braden did spend time that weekend discussing their wedding, houses and the future. Braden could hardly be kept from the subject. But invariably his plans were so grandiose Chloe couldn't picture herself in the kind of life he wanted for them.

"*Five* bridesmaids," she cried. "Where would I even *find* five bridesmaids?"

"My parents' close friends have daughters. There's Chris and David Trassault's daughter, your friends from Pentwater. I don't think five is a great number. I went to a wedding once with ten."

"We have certainly gone to different weddings," Chloe said. "I just want a small wedding in our church and ..."

"Your church couldn't hold all the people we would need to invite. My parents have suggested a large church they know of in Chicago. They've gone to many weddings there. Look. I even have a picture of it."

Chloe looked at the picture doubtfully.

"It's certainly an impressive building. But what religion is it?"

"I don't know," Braden said. "Why does that matter?"

"It matters to *me*," Chloe said, "because a church isn't just a building. It's a place where people of similar beliefs worship God."

"We could get your pastor to perform the ceremony there."

155

"Thanks, Braden," Chloe said, giving his hand a squeeze. "I'm sure he'd be agreeable. That would be a comfort."

"See how accommodating I am?" Braden said proudly.

But Chloe felt like she was being pulled off her feet and propelled into a world she was a stranger to. This, of course, was Braden's world, the only one he knew. *Heaven knows he grew up in a palace*, she thought. The differences in their upbringing, not important while dating each other, looked more formidable to Chloe now.

"My mother can't wait to take you shopping for your wedding dress in Chicago. She says there are only four designers she trusts. They insist on doing the attendant dresses as well so the looks don't clash."

"Hmmm," Chloe said. "I can't believe you are into dress designing, Braden."

"I'm not," Braden replied. "I work with buildings. My mother is into dresses."

"But you remember so well what she said."

"I'm a detail person. I can't help it," Braden said cheerily.

Chloe sighed, unwilling to say more for fear of starting another disagreement. Braden looked at her intently.

"You're not worried about the cost, are you? I hope *that's* not what makes you look so glum. My parents insist on paying for the entire wedding."

"Oh, Braden, I couldn't ask them to do that."

"As I said, they insist. I am their only progeny. They have only one occasion to host a wedding, and they want to make the most of it."

"How many people?" Chloe asked suspiciously.

"A lot; business associates, extended family, friends, whatever. What does it matter?"

"I'll be scared to death."

Braden took her in his arms, kissing her forehead gently.

"Just close your eyes and jump, sweetie. One day

and then it will be just you and I. Then we'll go hide in some tropical paradise for a week. I'd say two, but I have to be back at work."

"It just doesn't seem like me," Chloe said dully.

"You can handle it. Be brave. Most women would give anything for such a wedding. You wait. In two years you'll be a society maven in Chicago, spending your husband's money like crazy and loving every minute of it."

"But I thought you didn't like that type of woman," Chloe reminded him.

Braden looked a little startled. He thought about that one for a minute.

"I *did* say that. But you'll always be the same *inside* where it counts."

"Just a more polished veneer added, like a house?" Chloe shot back with irony.

Braden ignored the barb.

"Yeah. You can take the girl out of Pentwater, but you can't take Pentwater out of the girl."

"You're incorrigible," sniffed Chloe. "But now I'm done. No more wedding talk. I know it's bitter out. But such sassiness as yours can only be cured by a walk on the beach."

"In this weather?"

"Definitely," Chloe said. "Get on your jacket."

18 RACE TO CHRISTMAS

Chloe wished time would stand still. Lately the sand in the hourglass of her life was pouring out faster and faster, propelling her into the unknown, and she didn't like it. Lilli was as bouncy as a Mexican jumping bean about seeing her father again at Christmas. Chloe marveled at how Lilli accepted change, with hardly a look back, while she ... was she really so old and set in her ways?

She saw Mark regularly at church, usually with Braden in tow. Braden made it a point to acknowledge Mark and shake his hand in passing, enjoying the victory. Mark was unfailingly gloomy in their presence. However, Chloe had the feeling Braden was alert to Mark's importance, bringing his name up warily on occasion. Chloe calmed his doubts at these times, hardly liking to think of Mark at all.

In church Mark was a common fixture. He ushered and greeted in addition to being a youth leader. He must be doing a good job, Chloe thought. Lilli enjoyed going to the meetings, often with Melanie tagging along. Chloe saw him talking to Marcie Turner frequently and wondered if they were now a steady duo.

"I don't know how he can stand her," Chloe thought with a touch of bitterness, all the while realizing she was being unfair. Though they didn't seem right together, it was Marcie's obvious admiration of Mark that rankled. Though Mark had been dismissive of Marcie, had he changed his mind? Chloe knew it shouldn't make a particle of difference to her, but it did—it did.

Sometimes, if she was alone, Mark looked as though he would speak to her if she gave him any encouragement. But Chloe was careful to avoid this by a quick nod of the head and a rapid exit.

Why does Mark always bring me pain? she thought. She found thoughts of him only heightened the confusion she was experiencing in her life at present. If she saw Mark walking down the street or in a store— and this had happened a few times in the weeks before Christmas—she would duck down another aisle or turn down another street to avoid him. *I have to stay focused on my life, on my wedding,* she thought. And seeing Mark made her lose this focus.

Plans for the wedding were inexorably taking shape, with a date set for late May. Chloe convinced Braden the weather would be "too cold" before then, a convenient stall. Her fears of leaving Pentwater and of marriage in general were being swallowed up by the "hulking monster" of the wedding itself. Apparently, it "had" to be a mammoth event held in an enormous church with a massive banquet afterward for hundreds of people who "must attend."

Braden, at his mother's direction, plied her with samples of menus, photographs from various photographers, wedding invitations, decorations, dresses, flowers, even hairstyles. Chloe realized that this would be Braden's mother's wedding, planned and funded by his parents. Though Chloe was allowed the final say in most areas, her choices were limited to what was presented to her. And after a few attempts at letting her opinions be known led to arguments with Braden, Chloe "rolled with the flow" and tried to forget about the huge extravaganza she would be the center of in May. Of course, at times this was difficult. And many times, after Braden left for Chicago, Chloe craved time alone on the bleak, ever-more-wintry beach, to be alone with her thoughts and to find herself again, which was becoming harder and harder to do.

One particularly difficult Monday morning around the middle of December, after one of these walks, Pops caught Chloe coming in the door with tears streaming down her face.

"Chloe, what's wrong?"

"Oh, nothing," Chloe said, dabbing at her cheeks with a handkerchief. "This wedding is getting to me, is all. Braden and his mother want a three-ring circus."

"Is it just the wedding you're concerned about? You know the Willises *do* attach importance to such things. It's only one day, after all."

"I know," Chloe replied, trying to compose herself. "I don't know. It's just ... everything; leaving home for Chicago, getting married. Oh, Pops, I'm so confused."

Pops looked thoughtful. "Lots of people have pre-wedding jitters. Changing your life is difficult at first. Could it be that? Or do you think it's something deeper?"

"Maybe I'm too old and resistant to change."

"At 27? Hardly," Pops said with a smile. "The hoopla of the wedding will pass, you know."

"And then I'm stuck in Chicago for the rest of my life," Chloe said, grimacing.

"Chloe," Pops said, "nobody said you had to marry Braden or get married at all."

"That's the trouble," moaned Chloe. "I think I'm in love with Braden. He's kind of addictive."

Pops laughed in spite of himself. "Well, that's the oddest description of love I've heard yet, an addiction. But you can't have it both ways. And I'm pretty sure a fellow like Braden wouldn't want to settle here."

"Oh, I know. We're as far apart as the North and South Pole, I'm afraid."

"Then either find a meeting place in between or don't marry," Pops said.

"Well, the wedding ball is rolling now," Chloe said. "It's getting so big I'm afraid it will roll me over if I try to stop it."

"Oh, pshaw," Pops said, patting Chloe's shoulder. "Weddings are canceled every day. I have confidence in you, Chloe. I know you'll make the right decision."

With Christmas only a week and a half away, Chloe had her hands full getting Manitou Inn ready for the holidays. Though they always decorated, this year, with all their "new" family coming, Chloe cast a jaundiced eye on the fraying ribbon and bows they had used for the banisters, as well as other well-worn decorations of years past.

"We need to put up something different this year," Chloe said to Pops. "And what on earth am I going to get David and Chris Trassault, their children and the Willises for Christmas? To say nothing of Braden."

Pops, a typical man, had little sympathy with such matters.

"Why do you have to get them anything at all? I'm sure they don't expect or need anything. And I think the decorations look fine. Some are a little old. But so what?"

"Oh, Pops, Manitou Inn has been mostly empty other Christmases. It was fine for you, me and Lilli. But this year I want it to look especially nice."

Pops, with a second look at Chloe's anxious face, said soothingly, "Take a couple days off. Go to Grand Rapids to shop. Buy what you need. What better way spend our money? Write down your menus. I'll get Maude going on the food while you're gone. But don't look so worried, Chloe. Don't lose the Christmas spirit in all your preparations. Remember, Christmas is the celebration of Jesus' birth. And *that's* what's important, period."

Chloe gulped. "I know. But I needed that reminder. We *are* entertaining big this year, however. And I can't help feeling a little nervous."

Pops took Chloe in his arms and hugged her tightly, something he had done frequently in childhood but not as often in her adult years.

"Chloe, I can see you're under a lot of stress lately. But just take it easy. Things will work out the way they're meant to. You'll see. Pray, praise God, and try to stay calm so you can listen to the direction he gives you. Trust in God to lead you through this and he will."

"I know," Chloe said, nestling against Pops' chest. "He's never let us down, has he, Pops?"

"No. And we've seen bad times, haven't we, dear?"

"Yes."

"And yet here we are, safe and sound in his care."

Chloe managed a smile.

"Thanks, Pops. I'll go straight to bed now and drive to Grand Rapids tomorrow to get our glorious Christmas underway. If you don't mind, I'll stay in a hotel and shop for two full days."

"That's fine. And don't worry about expense, Chloe. We have so much to celebrate this year."

"We do," Chloe agreed, smiling as she thought of Lilli. "Now I'm happy again."

The next day, with a gray December sky spitting a mixture of snow and slushy sleet, Chloe drove one and a half hours to Grand Rapids, a larger city to the south of Pentwater, where the brightly decorated mall with its elegant merchandise cheered her. Though she was normally careful with money, Chloe went through her list at full throttle. She bought bright ribbons, holiday candles, lawn decorations, tree ornaments and table trimmings to make Manitou Inn glitter this Christmas. Next came Lilli's requests and new reading material for

Pops. After some thought, Chloe decided on fine chocolate, cheeses, jams and other delicacies for the Willises and Traussalts, combined with some of Lilli's paintings, which she knew she could have framed in Pentwater by a client of hers who had a framing shop. The problem of Braden's gift she solved by a gold key chain engraved with his initials and "Love, Chloe" on the back.

That's the best I can do, she thought. *He has everything else.*

Later that night in the hotel, Chloe hurriedly wrapped her gifts from the day so, when she returned to Pentwater, her car was filled with wrapped and unwrapped goodies.

"You look like Old St. Nick himself," Pops said after his tenth run to her car for more Christmas treasures. "You outdid yourself. But you're right. This Christmas is uniquely joyful, and Manitou Inn has to reflect that joy."

"Yes," Chloe said breathlessly, carrying in two bags. "Now I have a week to get everything in place and clean. We'll have to spread plastic where the workers are to keep their dust out."

"Done," Pops said. "Now I'm feeling the excitement too."

Lilli, coming home from school, made a beeline for the packages. Luckily Chloe had time to store Lilli's presents in a "safe spot." So she knew Lilli's search would be in vain.

"Oh, Chloe," Lilli said, gently holding up some lighted angels Chloe had bought for the front yard, "these are soooo pretty. I hope it snows for Christmas. Won't that be perfect?"

"Yes, sweetie, it will."

"My dad is coming and Chris and my brother and sister. Has there ever been a better Christmas?"

"Never," Chloe admitted. "But then every Christmas

is special because we have Jesus and I have you."

"I know," Lilli said, jumping into Chloe's lap, something she had not done of late. "I love you, Chloe," she whispered.

"I love you too, honey," Chloe replied, her eyes tearing. "You're truly my Christmas angel."

"Thanks," Lilli said. And kissing Chloe on the cheek, she jumped up again.

"Lilli," Chloe said, calling her back, "Don't you think it would be nice to give your father, Chris, brother, sister and even the Willises a picture of yours? We would frame them, of course."

Lilli stopped in her tracks, turned towards Chloe again and excitedly clapped her hands. "That's great," she said. "I'll look for some now. They'll have to be my best ones."

Chloe smiled. Now she felt at peace. Her Christmas dreams were coming true—or at least moving along nicely.

19 CHRISTMAS

Lilli got her wish. The three days before Christmas saw softly drifting snow that covered Pentwater like a down comforter. It was the first substantial snowfall of the season. And no drifts of dirty snow packed in huge banks by snowplows were to be seen. Pentwater was a picture postcard.   And Manitou Inn's lawn angels blinked serenely in the mellowing dusk.

Lilli, dressed in a swishy satin dress of red plaid, her dark hair pulled back from her face with red and green ribbons, looked a Christmas picture herself. She leaned over the living room sofa, heating the window with her breath while gazing at the street, impatiently awaiting the arrival of her guests. It was Christmas Eve at 5:00 o'clock.

"Oh, Chloe, where are they? We have to be at church at 7:00."

"I know, honey. But both the Trassaults and Willises said 5:30. Their plane should be landed by now. In fact, I'm expecting a call ..."

The phone's ringing interrupted her. Chloe picked up the phone breathlessly.

"Merry Christmas, darling," boomed Braden's voice. "We're on the ground. We've met the Trassaults. You should be seeing all of us soon."

"Be careful, Braden. We're anxiously awaiting you here," Chloe said, glancing in Lilli's direction.

Manitou Inn's quiet burst to life when the door opened to the Trassaults and Willises a half an hour later. They had met on the plane. So introductions were unnecessary. Everyone was talking at once and seemed in fine spirits. Chloe, with Braden's arms around her waist, enjoyed Lilli's excitement at meeting her new brother and sister for the first time. Lilli was hugging everyone and as animated as Chloe had ever seen her. Elaine and Joseph Trassault warmed quickly to Lilli's exuberance. In fact, it wasn't an exaggeration to say that they, like Lilli, were in a joyous mood.

"Mom, I swear, doesn't Lilli look like me at her age?" Elaine enthused.

"You could be twins," Chris said with a laugh.

Tall Joseph airlifted Lilli and dangled her in front of him with clumsy affection.

"You coming to see me at college, kid?" he said gruffly.

"Yes, yes, yes," Lilli cried merrily.

"Watch out, Joe, or you'll wreck her dress," Elaine scolded, reaching up to snatch Lilli from her brother's arms.

"Come on, everybody, it's out the door. You heard Chloe say church is at 7:00," Chris reminded them. "Let's celebrate Christmas at God's house first."

In church, Chloe experienced the true wonder of Christmas. Amidst the softly glowing candles that brightened the darkness, the minister's oft-repeated story of the birth of Christ and the singing of beautiful Christmas carols, Chloe's Christmas was complete. Singing with a loud, happy voice, she looked up to see Mark staring at her from the front of church where he was helping with Communion.

A lump formed in Chloe's throat, and she wanted to cry. *Everything would be so perfect,* she thought, *if only*

... but then she shook her head, making sure she did not look in Mark's direction again. *I'm not going to let the ghosts of Christmases past spoil my joy this year,* Chloe thought stubbornly, though she remembered her two angels, Marie and her mother, in prayer.

Back at Manitou Inn, presents were scattered under the tree. Lilli hovered around them, jiggling and locating each of hers. Maude had outdone herself. There were two plates of cold appetizers, hot mulled cider and an assortment of home-baked Christmas cookies. Everyone was happily chattering. When Chloe looked for Braden's parents, she found them sitting primly on one of the couches, carefully balancing plates on their knees. They sipped the mulled cider and didn't say much, smiling elegantly once in awhile. Chloe couldn't help noticing their condescending looks as they took in Manitou Inn.

They're used to better, she thought. *What about Braden? Did he have the same patronizing attitude? No. He looked happy. But would he soon turn into a junior version of his parents, looking down his nose at anything not done on a grand scale?* Chloe knew she should be more understanding. But the thought stuck sourly in her mind. *And what about me? What will I be in 10 years? A society maven as Braden suggested?* The idea was repellent to Chloe. Indeed, the very thought of her future in Chicago could, if she let it, cast a shadow on this, her most wonderful of Christmases.

I'll put my trust in God and let him guide me through this. It was becoming apparent that, if she was having these thoughts amidst the holiday gaiety going on around her, a serious problem *did* exist and would have to be dealt with and soon. How to deal with it, however, Chloe had no clue. *That's why I'm turning it over to God in prayer.* With that consoling thought, Chloe turned her attention back to her guests.

Throughout the evening, it was evident that Braden's

parents *did* relish the idea of an acquaintance with David Traussalt and his wife. Chloe could see—and was in part grateful—that they also appeared pleased with Lilli—or her talent at least. They apparently had "shown off" the picture of Lilli's Chloe had given them for Thanksgiving to many of their friends, who were amazed that it came from the palette of an 8-year-old.

From Christmas Eve on Thursday until 4:00 p.m. on Sunday, when their guests bid Manitou Inn goodbye and headed to the airport for their flight back to Chicago, the Inn was filled with Henings, Trassaults and Willises feasting, opening presents, attempting to cross country ski on the freshly fallen snow and even helping Lilli build her first snowman of the season. For the number of people intermingling and their previous lack of acquaintance, Chloe was amazed the holiday passed with such joy and a definite "together" feeling between the families.

"Wow, everybody gets along so well," Braden enthused to Chloe, arching his eyebrows significantly. "And you were so worried." His look seemed to be saying that Chloe's concerns about their upcoming marriage and moving to Chicago would disappear as well.

But when everyone left, Chloe became so dejected she burst into tears while picking up dishes hours after Pops and Lilli had retired for the night. *I'm just exhausted,* she thought to herself, heading for her room at last. *I'll go to bed. I'll be fine in the morning.*

20 THE SNOWSTORM

But the next day, Monday, Chloe's mood didn't improve and the weather seemed to echo it. Increasing winds drove the snow down in sheets, unlike the softly falling flakes of the holiday weekend. Why she was melancholy Chloe hardly dared to think. In her heart perhaps she had expected the warm emotions of Christmas to magically solve those worries and fears she had been enduring lately. Unfortunately, this was not the case, and they still loomed as dark shadows in her mind. The family area of Manitou Inn, still cluttered from its holiday guests, seemed oppressive to Chloe. Lilli had left for Melanie's in the morning, her favorite Christmas presents in her backpack, for a day and night of play and, truth be told, serious bragging about her new family. She would not return until Tuesday. Pops napped on the sofa and read the paper all morning and, in the afternoon, left for the hotel area to supervise the few workers who had straggled in to work on the renovation.

Chloe sat down at her desk, determined to make some progress on her accounts but, after ten minutes of staring at the same page, gave up. Her concentration was zero today. She got to her feet and gazed out the window at the whiteness.

I have to get out of here or I'll go crazy, she thought. Chloe knew her face reflected her low spirits, and she could feel a crying jag coming on. So, to avoid facing Pops and his concern, Chloe hurriedly scribbled a note that she was going for a drive and left it on the kitchen table where Pops would find it. She swiftly threw on her jacket, hat and mittens and waded through the snow to her car. After removing the drifts of snow that covered her vehicle, Chloe slipped into the driver's seat and started the engine. Its welcoming growl enervated her, giving her some sense of control, a feeling sorely lacking in her life lately. Chloe turned the car towards the road that ran along the beach. Though the sand was shrouded in a blanket of snow, Lake Michigan had not frozen over. Chloe longed for the power and continuity of the gray waves pounding the shore. *I'll feel better then*, she thought. *And maybe I can do some straight thinking.*

Forced to concentrate on the snowy road ahead of her, Chloe found the challenge lifted her spirits. She drove some distance before stopping on the side of the road to watch the snow whip over the lake's raging breakers. It was a world of white and fierce gray waters. Chloe sat in silence, watching the beauty of winter. After a time, as dusk darkened the sky, Chloe reluctantly turned her car around and headed back to Manitou Inn. *I haven't solved my problems*, she thought. *But I do feel more at peace.*

As she drove, however, the snow worsened, becoming so thick the windshield wipers couldn't wipe it away. Chloe inched on blindly, feeling for the side of the road with her right tires. There was no traffic on the road and, unfortunately, no lights to guide her. Her headlights were useless. The snow deflected their light into her eyes. *I hope I'm on the road,* she thought worriedly.

Suddenly there was a "thud" and the car stopped, its wheels spinning. Chloe pushed the door open to find she had run into a sand dune on the side of the road. She got back in, throwing the car into reverse. But the combination of slick snow and the still-soft sand that engulfed her right front tire held it fast. Then the left front tire sunk into a rut. The more Chloe attempted to back the car out, the deeper her tires embedded themselves in the dune. Chloe tried everything she could think of. She placed blankets in back of the tires and struggled to push the car backwards. But nothing worked.

Now I have something to cry about, Chloe thought. *I can't believe I was stupid enough to go out in a snowstorm when I know how bad lake-effect snow can be.* Covered with snow that was melting in the warmth of the car, Chloe pulled out her cell phone and dialed Manitou Inn's number with shaking fingers.

"Pops, Pops, can you hear me?" Chloe shouted into the receiver. The storm was causing static on her cell phone.

"Chloe," she heard Pops' voice say, going in and out of connection. "Where are you?"

"On the beach road. I'm stuck," Chloe replied.

"Where?" Pops' voice was becoming fainter.

"A ways out, I think. I'm at least eight miles from Pentwater."

Whether Pops heard her or not, Chloe didn't know. His voice cut off completely, leaving only static. Chloe kept calling Manitou Inn—and 911—but got nothing. Then her phone battery died. *I forgot to charge it over the holidays,* Chloe thought, *how foolish.* She sat in the car, its heat on, wondering what she should do next. Hopefully someone would come along, a snowplow or just another car. But the road remained deserted. An hour or so passed. The sky was now completely black. Chloe grew more frightened. Her phone was dead. And the gas tank read just above empty. Chloe knew the car wouldn't stay warm through the night, and snow was still falling at an alarming rate. *It's going to bury my car,* Chloe thought. She jumped out, using her windshield scraper and finally her arms to try to remove the snow that was engulfing her car.

It was hopeless. Chloe was afraid snow plugging the exhaust pipe would asphyxiate her if she stayed in the car. Or else she could fall asleep, lose consciousness and freeze. She made a decision to walk back towards Pentwater, following the road. She thought she saw a farmhouse on her way out. If she could make it there, she could call Pops again. *Any sign of civilization,* she thought, *would be welcome now.*

She took a deep breath and plunged into the storm. The winds struck her full force, sending her reeling against the car. The snow made it difficult to breathe. With an effort, Chloe stood up and trudged out. Her car disappeared in the whiteness almost immediately. Luckily, there were posts stuck every few yards alongside the road. She followed the road from post to post. Growing colder and more exhausted, Chloe began counting the posts to stay alert. She was up to 20 posts when thoughts of laying down came. *I can't do that,* Chloe thought, *or I'll never make it.* Each step forward was more difficult than the last. And just as Chloe felt she could go no farther, she saw two headlights coming towards her, illuminating the shower of snow.

I'm either hallucinating or that's a truck, Chloe thought. *But I'm going to assume it's real.* The lights got closer. Chloe stayed on the side of the road, waving her arms frantically. She feared the driver might not see her and mow her down. As the truck slowly passed, Chloe reached out and tapped on its front door. The small pickup truck slowed and stopped a few feet beyond her.

"Oh, that worked. Thank you, God," Chloe murmured.

The driver stepped out. Chloe weaved toward him.

"Mark," she whispered faintly. "How did you find me?"

Mark reached for her, holding her close.

"I can't believe I found you, Chloe! You have terrified your father and me!"

Chloe clung to him, her knees buckling with exhaustion and relief.

"I ... I'm sorry," she said in a shaky voice. "I just thought ... a drive down the beach and ..."

"In the middle of a winter storm. Not too smart," he said, carefully brushing the snow off Chloe's hat, coat and jeans. "Do you know how lucky we both are that I found you?"

"How did you know I was gone?" Chloe asked, her voice still quivering from fatigue.

"Your dad called me, frantic. You had called him. He heard the work 'stuck' but not much else. Then the connection went dead. He thought I might know where you'd gone—our old 'haunts,' so to speak. I'm glad he called me. It would not be good if he had come looking for you himself."

"I know," Chloe said, shivering as Mark bundled her into the truck. "Thank you, Mark."

"We'd better let him know you're safe," Mark said, climbing into the driver's seat of the truck. "Luckily, *my* cell phone is charged." He called the number—Chloe could see he still knew it by heart—and handed her the phone.

"Hello, hello?" Chloe could hear the tension in Pops' voice even through the static on the line.

"Pops, it's me, Chloe. I'm all right."

"Oh, thank God," Chloe heard Pops' exhale of relief. Then he said, "Why did you take off in a storm like that, Chloe? It's not like you to be so careless."

Chloe started to cry weakly, her tears flowing down her icy face.

"I'm so sorry to worry you, Pops. I was just depressed and ..."

"Say no more. Just tell that Mark to bring you back in one piece." Pops paused. "And thank him for me, will you?"

"But what about my car?"

"We'll get a tow truck out tomorrow when the storm subsides. Besides, who cares about a car next to you?"

"I love you, Pops. We'll come right home."

Luckily the pickup truck had four-wheel drive. Otherwise, Chloe and Mark stood a good chance of getting stuck again. Mark carefully maneuvered the truck around in the direction of Pentwater. They crept back toward town amidst howling winds and driving snow.

Mark had Chloe take off her wet jacket. Then he wrapped two heavy blankets around her. The new warmth made Chloe sleepy. Her head kept nodding. She didn't argue when Mark gently settled her head on his shoulder. The heat felt wonderful. The next thing Chloe knew was the truck coming to a stop in front of Manitou Inn. Her still-cold hands clumsily grasped the door's handlebar in an attempt to get out.

"Stay there, Chloe," Mark said. He came around to her side, opened the door and lifted her up in his arms. He carried her through the front door, which Pops had flung open for him.

"Bring her to the sofa," Pops said. Chloe saw Pops had made a cocoon of blankets on the sofa, and Mark draped them around her.

"I'm okay," Chloe protested.

"No, you're not," Pops said gently but so firmly that both Chloe and Mark looked at him with surprise.

"I don't think she's frostbitten," Mark said.

"I can still feel my toes," Chloe added, wiggling them gingerly.

"That's not what I meant. When I found you had left the house during a winter storm, Chloe, I blamed myself because I know you've been upset lately and I haven't been of much help to you."

"Pops, not in front of Mark."

"No," Pops replied significantly. "Who better to tell

your troubles to than an old friend who has known you from childhood?"

"Chloe, what's the matter?" Mark asked, sitting next to Chloe on the sofa.

"Oh, Pops, I don't want to involve Mark in my problems."

But Pops just gave her a meaningful look.

"Sometimes we have to 'come clean' both to ourselves and others to make a bad situation right. And now, seeing that you're better *physically*, my dear, I'll leave you two alone to talk." And with that, Pops walked up the stairs to his room.

When they were alone, Mark sat next to Chloe and took both her hands in his.

"What's wrong, Chloe?"

Chloe looked away from him, fighting back tears.

"Pops shouldn't have said anything to you, Mark."

Then she quickly glanced back at him.

"What *did* he tell you, anyway?"

"Chloe, I promise you," Mark replied, holding her hands tighter as she tried to pull them away. "I promise you I know nothing more than what your father said just now."

"Well, he said enough, enough that you think I'm a fool."

"Because you're upset? Being sad doesn't make you a fool. The fact is I'm upset too. I'm miserable without you. I'm miserable you're with Braden. No. Your father loves you, Chloe. *I* love you. I wish you'd believe in me, Chloe, and believe that I've loved you always."

Mark's hands released Chloe's and cupped her face, forcing her to face him. She looked at him and, once she did, couldn't look away. They gazed at each other, stretching each second into an eternity. Then Mark reached for her and held her close.

"But what about Braden? What about the wedding?" Chloe sobbed, her cheek against Mark's shirt. "It's all settled. Braden doesn't deserve to be treated that way.

Besides, none of this would have happened if you hadn't left me in the first place."

"Of course it wouldn't have," Mark replied. "But it took that to make me realize how much I love you. It took that for me to realize the direction of my life. Now I know what happens when you live your live contrary to the Lord. Don't punish me—or yourself—any more, Chloe. I've suffered without you too, sometimes without even knowing it. My life has had a large empty hole in it ever since I left Pentwater. Sure, you can make the same mistake I did. You can marry Braden Willis and live in Chicago. But is that what you want? Will that make you happy? I hope and pray you won't come to realize too late, like I did, how special our love is. If you are determined to marry Braden, I can't stop you. But you have to tell me that," Mark said, still holding her tightly, "or I'll never let you go."

He slipped a finger under Chloe's chin, raising her tear-stained face to his.

"Do you love Braden, Chloe? Do you love him more than me?"

"Mark, stop," Chloe said, breaking free of his grasp. "I can't hurt Braden. I can't."

"Then tell him the truth," Mark said quietly. "He deserves that from you, and so do I."

"You don't ..." Chloe began angrily. But then she stopped. What was the use of staying angry with Mark any more if what he said was true? *Can anyone deny their own heart?* she thought. Chloe sat down on the couch and wrapped herself in a ball, her hands covering her face, as if to block out Mark and what he was saying. All the while a light and a release was beginning to grow inside her, a joyousness she stubbornly tried to deny. *Here is your solution,* her heart whispered. *Why fight it anymore?*

"You can leave any time," she told Mark, muffled inside her cocoon.

"I'm not going anywhere," Mark replied obstinately,

"until I get my answer." He moved closer to her. "Chloe ..." His lips were on her hair, her cheeks. Then Chloe raised her head and their lips met. Chloe felt such relief and happiness exploding inside her she could hardly bear it. She wrapped her arms around him and clung to him. How long it had been. She couldn't believe the feeling, like coming home after a long time away.

"You won't be leaving for Chicago," Mark whispered through her hair. "And don't worry. I will never leave you again."

The next morning Pops looked up from his coffee and smiled at Chloe, disheveled from the first sound sleep she'd had in weeks and with a brilliant smile on her face.

"Well," he said slyly, "looks like God answered your prayers after all!"

ABOUT THE AUTHOR

I've lived in Michigan all my life. With its inland lakes, charming lakeside towns, lighthouses and sandy beaches, Michigan is a perfect place for romance and adventure.

Pentwater is a small town with a beautiful harbor, windswept beaches and dunes nestled on Lake Michigan's shore. My family and I enjoyed many languid summer days there, caught in the ever-changing moods of the Big Lake.